HUNTED

AN URBAN FANTASY

ANN GIMPEL

CONTENTS

HUNTED
WAYWARD MAGE BOOK TWO

An Urban Fantasy

By
Ann Gimpel

Tumble off reality's edge into a dangerous world fueled by lore and magic

Copyright Page

BOOK DESCRIPTION: HUNTED

Learn magic they said. Or at least shore up your paltry skills. Talk is cheap, and that edict has cost me dearly.

I had a comfortable life, once upon a time. A quiet life. One where I'd carved a realistic niche for myself. No more. Power is seductive, and a bitch of a mistress. Once I pulled the cork out of that bottle, a million genies sallied forth.

None of them were nice. No one offered me three wishes, or any wishes at all. I've been working my fanny off for the last two years. Most days, I slog along from dawn to dusk and beyond. Sleep has turned into a distant memory. When I do lie down—or fall on my face, which is what really happens—my mind whirls in circles as I relive the failures *du jour*.

And the very occasional success.

I am stronger. So much stronger it scares me. My talent sparkles, flowing bright and clean. Soon, I'll leave the well-hidden spot that's allowed me time to claim what's mine.

Whether my crash course in sorcery was wise remains to be seen.

BOOKS IN THE WAYWARD MAGE SERIES

Hands of Fate (a novella)
Jinxed
Hunted
Salvaged

CHAPTER 1
ABRIA

Dip. Weave. Whirl. Fire flickered from the fingertips of my right hand. My left controlled air. This exercise always reminded me of dragons with judicious use of air fanning flames and turning them into a blowtorch.

When I thought I had the air part down, I switched things up and summoned water. As usual, the trickle I requested showed up as a tidal wave drenching me with cold, salty water.

Huffing and blowing, I let my spell go to wipe water out of my eyes and pounded a fist into the dirt wall. *Ouch.*

"Fuck!"

My practice arena was far underground and impeccably warded. I'd love to claim credit for the ward, but Cailleach had shaped and formed it. Because it never faltered, she had to be funneling a constant stream of magic into its weave.

Cailleach, crone goddess of winter, witches, and the sea

had taken an interest in me. Like everything in magical realms, having her for a teacher has been a mixed bag. She's wise, knowledgeable, and occasionally tolerant. She's also impatient with a short fuse. I'm not a witch, but she wouldn't have treated one of them any differently.

Actually, she did—treat them differently, that is—since she's never taken the time to guide any witch's magical ability. I wouldn't have known, except she screamed the information in my face one particularly difficult day when I'd accused her of handling me with less respect than she'd have afforded one of her kin.

The flood of seawater I'd inadvertently summoned had developed a life of its own. Rather than settling into a quiet pool, it formed small whitecaps ebbing and flowing like a miniature tide.

Grappling for the water end of power, I spun a different enchantment and commanded, "Stop that."

Nothing happened. A sigh pushed past my lips before I twisted them into a grimace. Once I formed something magical, altering its structure required a whole lot of work. It would be simpler to start over, but I had to get rid of this mess first.

"Never time to do it right, but there's always time to do it over," I mumbled and gathered my skill to try another tack.

Half an hour later, the white caps had moved from mid-calf to my knees. Somehow, I was making the problem worse. Water was far from my strongest suit, but still this was ridiculous. I'd had plans for today—supposedly, one of my last in residence with Cailleach—and so far I hadn't accomplished a thing.

I caught a whiff of witchy energy. Damn it. I'd hoped to have this predicament behind me before my taskmistress teacher showed up. I was making little shooing motions with both hands before I stopped myself. If none of the dozen spells I'd tried had any impact on the water level, shooing it into submission wouldn't work, either.

Cailleach's wasn't the only magic heading my way. I stopped, narrowed my eyes, and worked to identify what I sensed. The only ones who'd visited during my tenure here were unicorns, Blake—my Daoine Sidhe boyfriend—and Birgit, another witch who'd helped train me. Jethro, her familiar, had dropped by as well. He's a shifter seer and spends most of his time as an enormous black cat.

An idea poked me; I swapped things up. If I was about to have company, I'd much rather they assumed all the water was here at my behest. In a manner of speaking, it was. For now, I'd pretend I'd meant to create the mini inland sea.

Some things have grown easier. Safeguarding my thoughts is one of them. I tucked shielding around my mind to conceal my shame. If I couldn't even solve this simple problem, maybe I wasn't ready to leave after all.

I can't stay here forever.

Correct, but two years is nothing in mage time, I argued back.

Cailleach splashed toward me after ducking to clear the low lintel that served as entry to my workspace. She was half a head taller than me with a spare, bony build. Stark cheekbones, a high forehead, and a squared-off chin surrounded her beak of a nose. Tangled silver hair hung to her knees. Dressed in one of her many robes—this one a faded green—she looked like witches portrayed in children's books. All she needed was a pointy hat, a staff, and a cauldron to complete the picture.

Implacable fog-colored eyes settled on me. "What's all this?"

"I was, erm, experimenting." I resisted the urge to rock from foot to foot or squirm or do anything to suggest I was uncomfortable beneath her scrutiny.

"I can see that," she said dryly. "But what was the purpose of this…experiment?"

Standing straighter, I clasped my hands behind my back. "Water is my weakest element. I was testing various ways to enhance my control over it." I added a slight guileless smile. My words incorporated enough truth, she might believe me.

Colors swirled around her as she spun her unique brand of enchantment. Moments later, the water vanished, soaking into the dirt floor. Even if getting rid of it had worked for me, I'd have been left with a mud slick. Not Cailleach. The floor turned sandy, as if the water had never been here.

Her gaze returned to me; I steeled myself for the lecture I was certain sat on the tip of her tongue. It never materialized. Instead, she said, "You have visitors. Otherwise, I'd have made you tidy up your own chaos."

Oops. Guess she figured it out. Thank all the gods she wasn't in a mood to belabor my shortcomings. Or to stand over me until I finally got something right—no matter how many days it took.

To divert her attention away from my flaws and failings, I asked, "Visitors? Who?" Remembering the other magical signature I'd sensed, I searched but couldn't locate it.

"You'll see."

If I'd had hackles, they'd have risen the length of my spine. I didn't like surprises. I started to say I wasn't in the mood, but the words never made it beyond my throat. I've always been a loner—except for the animals, birds, fish, and insects who idolize me. People—magical and otherwise—never held much appeal, but I was lonely. I've never had this long a period of enforced solitude where even a trip to the corner market wasn't on the menu. There was no corner market. Supplies came from somewhere, but I had no say in what showed up or how it got here.

Cailleach has several dwellings. She's told me about a few of them. This compound, complete with a castle, moat, drawbridge, and portcullis, occupied a corner of a small borderworld not far from Earth. In addition to my workshop, I also had a bedchamber and access to an expansive library.

Suddenly self-conscious, I glanced down at my patched trousers, ancient T-shirt emblazoned with "Wolves Bite," and scuffed boots. "Should I change?" I didn't have anything nicer, but I could manage cleaner.

Before we'd ended up here, I'd gathered a few items from my home. I couldn't live there any longer; it wasn't safe. During my hasty egress, the winter goddess had created a quarter-hour window and told me to make efficient use of it.

Efficient equated to racing up the steep stairs to my

second-floor living quarters and tossing everything I could lay my hands on into a battered valise. Since I hadn't had time to pick and choose, I'd ended up with schlocky garments like my wolf T-shirt. Functional but far from stylish.

Cailleach's gray brows shot up; a small furrow formed between them. Clearly, changing clothes hadn't occurred to her. "Perhaps 'tis a decent idea. You're soaked, and 'twill save explanations."

I started to ask, "To whom?" Instead, I nodded and loped for the stairs beyond the cave's entrance. I'd already asked who these mysterious visitors were. She'd declined to answer. A second query would meet with the same fate.

A few minutes later, I was garbed in black slacks, a teal sweater, and a puffy black vest. Not wanting to take the time to comb out my mass of tangled hair, I scrunched it into an elastic band and headed for the castle's formal drawing room.

It was as good a place as any to start, but it turned out I guessed right. Moving quickly, I bolted into the room and screeched to a halt. It had been hundreds of years since I'd seen Ceridwen and Arianrhod, but I'd know the two goddesses anywhere.

"My ladies," I murmured and dropped into a deep curtsy. I've never been very good at them and swayed alarmingly until I regained my balance.

"For the love of Danu, get up," Ceridwen growled. She'd been sitting facing a roaring fire along with Arianrhod and Cailleach. Now, she stood over me. I hadn't seen her cross the vast room, but there she was in all her six-and-a-half-foot-plus splendor.

I rose, not sure what to say. "Nice to see you," seemed trite. "Been a long time," was banal as hell.

Ceridwen looked much the same. Tall and broad, she wore hunting leathers crafted from soft, pale doeskin with boots laced to knee level. Her eyes were dark, her forehead high. Black hair frosted with silver hung to her waist in multiple braids. The only thing missing was her cauldron, and I felt certain it had to be close. The goddess never went anywhere without it. Serving as the seat of her seer powers, it was an integral part of her energy.

Arianrhod joined her. About the same height, but with a lithe build, she too wore leather garments, but hers were crafted from darker-colored hide. She examined me from multi-hued eyes: one gold, the other silver. Hair like spun gold had been gathered into a bun at the nape of her neck. A bronze torc studded with turquoise circled her neck, and her hunting bow was secured across her back in a battered sheath.

Questions crowded the back of my mind; I sat on all of them. Had Cailleach sought them out? Seemed likely since so few people knew I was here. The weight of their combined gazes scoured me up one side and down the other. They were taking my measure, but the question was why.

"You've learned to hold your tongue," Ceridwen observed.

"Aye, that she has," Arianrhod agreed. "Particularly given what a chatty little thing she used to be."

That did it. I crossed my arms beneath my breasts and said, "I have never been *chatty*."

"Don't be argumentative." Ceridwen rebuked me.

"Aye, 'twould take very little to change our minds," Arianrhod chimed in.

"About what?" I tried for a neutral tone but ended up sounding snarky.

"Independent, isn't she?" Arianrhod muttered.

"I am not a *she*. I'm right here. And I'm..." It took a bit for me to do the math before continuing. "I'm over 700 years old. If I hadn't developed some independence in all that time, there truly would have been no hope for me."

Ceridwen's eyes widened. Arianrhod made a, "Tsk, tsk," clicking sound with her tongue against her teeth.

Oh-oh. I'd been rude. Cailleach didn't tolerate backtalk. Why would I expect anything different from the pair staring at me. The winter goddess rose from her seat in front of the fire. No wood here; magic powered these flames. It was one of the ways she'd taught me to control that element.

I expected her to order me out of the room—maybe out of her castle—but she didn't. That part would probably come later. After she'd chastised me for showing so little respect.

The cauldron I'd wondered about clattered down in front of Ceridwen. Just as I'd suspected, it had been sequestered somewhere close by. The liquid within bubbled and splattered on the tile floor. The goddess snatched a glass rod from the air, stirring and muttering.

When she looked up, she announced, "Naught has changed."

My tolerance for ambiguity has never been high. "Would someone please tell me what's going on?" I demanded.

Cailleach hurried to where the three of us stood and draped an arm around my shoulders. The gesture surprised me since she's never been affectionate. More of a business-as-usual type.

"You've known your time with me was drawing to an end," she said. At my nod, she went on, "Quite a while ago, Blake and I discussed the next steps in your training—"

"Without me?" I screeched before clapping a hand over my mouth and mumbling, "Sorry."

"Of course without you." Cailleach's tone was implacable. "What could you have possibly offered that might have been germane?"

I clasped my hands behind me to squelch a desire to punch her. What could I have possibly offered, huh? Oh nothing much since I was only the topic of their discussion.

"In any event," Cailleach went on. After all these months, she knew me well. Surely, she was aware of my inner turmoil, but she viewed it as an inconvenience, not anything worthy of being addressed.

"In any event, what?" I growled, tired of masking my irritation.

"The best choice to complete your magical induction is those who created you," she went on.

"But you were gone." I addressed Ceridwen and Arianrhod.

"Not so far gone Blake couldn't find us." Ceridwen grimaced.

"We'd forgotten what good trackers the Daoine Sidhe are. He cheated, though," Arianrhod added.

"Aye, his first stop was a little chat with the Morrigan in Hell," Ceridwen said.

"Not much incentive for her to keep her mouth shut." Arianrhod made a sour face.

It was as if they'd forgotten I was here. To fix that, I spoke up. "Blake would have found you anyway. Even without the Morrigan's help."

"What makes you so sure?" Ceridwen asked.

"He can be quite determined. And he's in love with me, which means he would have tried even harder than usual."

The goddess's mouth formed an O. She consulted her cauldron and muttered, "Interesting. I'd missed that bit of information."

She may have missed it, but Blake hadn't said a word to me. He could have. He was just here a fortnight ago. I'd take it up with him later.

Cailleach and Arianrhod were conversing telepathically. Power swirled around them. Ceridwen bent over her cauldron. I felt like an anachronism. My future had been decided behind my back. That Blake had been part of it hurt a lot.

They simply assumed I'd comply—with anything they outlined. We'd see about that. "No need to take me on as a project if you don't want to," I announced.

Three sets of startled eyes zeroed in on me.

"She does that," Cailleach said.

"Does what?" I was done being deferential. "Since when is speaking up for oneself a crime?" I blew out a breath.

"Never mind. Don't answer that. I can leave, return to Blake. He and I will figure this out."

"Testy little thing." Arianrhod settled her hands on her slender hips.

"Reminds me of you when you were young," Ceridwen said.

"Oh, really?" Arianrhod hooded her eyes.

Cailleach clapped her hands smartly. A tray bearing a silver teapot, cups, and spoons floated in from somewhere and settled on a nearby table. "Let's have a spot of tea, shall we?" she suggested brightly.

I snatched a mug and poured hot water over tea leaves. The heady fragrance of rosemary, mint, and lemongrass soothed me. Before my next words took shape, I grasped Cailleach's strategy. She meant to defuse the tension sitting thickly in her drawing room.

It worked.

"Sorry," I said. "I've never cared for surprises, and I've always needed to plan for change."

"Understood." Cailleach squeezed my shoulder and guided me toward a chair. "I know those things about you, and I should have said something."

I latched onto her gray gaze. Some realizations come too late, but this one arrived in time to do something about it. "You've been kind to me," I told her. "You took me in when you had no reason to. I haven't been an easy pupil, but you stuck it out."

A rare smile graced her gaunt face. "You're welcome."

I'd been looking forward to returning to Blake and Underhill, but now I wasn't in any rush to leave. My years with Cailleach were as close as I'd ever come to having a mother.

"Trust the process," she said into my mind. *"Everything will work out."*

Of course, the others heard her, but no one said a word. I knew without being told that once tea was over, I'd be on my way.

"Where will I go next?" I asked.

"We're working on that," Arianrhod said.

"Aye, our kinsmen aren't any more kindly disposed toward you than they were seven centuries ago," Ceridwen added.

The where of things had yet to be decided. I've always been good at problem ownership, so I moved on to practical elements. "Will I bring my things?"

"What kind of things?" Ceridwen asked.

I shrugged. "Just clothing."

Ceridwen's brows rose in twin question marks. Cailleach explained, "Abria is a natural. She doesn't require props to support her power."

"Told you." Ceridwen jerked her chin at Arianrhod. "She's a lot like you."

"Better than dragging that damnable kettle everywhere," Arianrhod retorted.

I fought back a smile. My earlier outrage at being treated like a mindless stick of furniture was fading. This would be like plopping into the middle of two battling sisters. If I was careful and didn't take sides, I might survive the experience.

CHAPTER 2
ABRIA

When I slipped out of the drawing room to toss my few garments into my valise, I fully expected we'd leave straightaway. First a day meandered by, and then a second. I returned to the main part of Cailleach's castle multiple times but couldn't locate a trace of the three goddesses.

Had Ceridwen and Arianrhod changed their minds? Was I to remain with Cailleach after all? I sent three messages to Blake in shielded telepathy, but he didn't answer. Maybe he was too far away. Hunching over my rucksack poised for departure felt pointless, so I went back to practicing magic.

I was in the library looking up a transmutation spell when a whoosh, flash, and bang spun me around with my hands raised. Power crackled from my fingertips. I was alone here, and I'd be damned if I'd be caught flatfooted if one of my many enemies breached Cailleach's defensive wards.

There'd been a time when I avoided conflict.

No more. That was the old me. The new me commanded boatloads more power. My latest watchword was to maim first and ask questions later. "Show yourself," I gritted and faced the spot the whoosh had originated. Adrenaline hummed along my nerve endings.

I felt strong. Invincible.

Watch it, a wise inner voice counseled. To date, all my practice had been just that: practice. Cailleach was tough, but I had yet to test my mettle against a real enemy.

The salt scent of the sea, rich, briny, and unmistakable, rolled through the library. Tension bled out of me. Cailleach had returned. Were the others with her?

I waited until the witch goddess oozed through a gash in the air, dark robes bunching around her. "Making good use of your time, I see." She came as close as she was capable to beaming at me.

"Trying." I smiled back.

What I didn't do was mention it would have been polite, considerate even, for her to tell me she'd be gone. Usually she left rows of runes drifting around the castle. They floated until they found me before dissipating. As she'd sagely noted, her method filled two gaps. It taught me the common runic alphabet as well as alerting me if she wouldn't be in residence for a while.

I stared around and behind her, but neither Arianrhod nor Ceridwen appeared. Questions clamored at the base of my throat. I swallowed them all. If there was information to be bandied about, the goddess would fill me in as she chose.

I'd thought I was prepared to leave her tutelage, but the relief sluicing through me suggested otherwise. I'd carved out a comfortable niche here, and I was loathe to trade it for any amount of time with the Celts. They'd never been kind. Never paid me any heed at all. They'd had their reasons, but knowing those reasons didn't make their indifference sting any less.

And then there was the niggling issue of my future being decided for me. Whining about a lack of autonomy was foolish. My power might be stronger, but when balanced against the Celts' or Cailleach's, I was still the greenest of neophytes.

Fully corporeal, Cailleach waved a bony index finger in front of my face. "Not getting off the hook that easily." She smirked.

Rats. I tightened up the warding I held around my mind, but she had a way of drilling through my best efforts.

A high-pitched trill left the goddess's throat. I recognized the summons and walked to a long table. Carved from dark wood, it spanned the length of the generous room. Books and scrolls lined every wall. As I'd expected, platters of food materialized, along with goblets overflowing with mead.

All right. We were going to eat first. Did it bode ill? Was she working on lowering my guard before she dropped a bombshell? Feigning nonchalance—after all, it was only my immediate future at stake—I picked and chose succulent bits of meat, cheese, pickles, and olives. Fresh bread provided a platform for the other items.

Cailleach sat across from me. We ate in silence for a few minutes before she said, "I suppose you wondered where we went."

She hadn't asked a question, so I offered a noncommittal grunt and went on eating. I really was hungry. I'd been living on nuts and chocolate since the goddesses left. Not for any specific reason other than sheer laziness, I kept a stash of nibbles in my bedchamber. Eating what was in front of me had been simpler than conjuring up something more nutritious.

Cailleach tapped a long nail on the scarred tabletop. "The problem," she went on, "was where to take you."

"I'm good with staying here," I blurted.

"Of course you would be, but I've taught you enough. The world hasn't been quiescent while you've stepped aside. You'll require all your talents and more to fulfill your role."

My eyebrows shot up. "What role?"

A slight shrug. "Not my place to tell you."

My earlier smile had faded. "If not yours, than whose?"

"That remains to be seen." She cleared her throat and took a hefty swallow from her goblet. "Meanwhile, I'm to deliver you to your next station once we've eaten."

"Where might that be?"

"Does it matter?" Colorless eyes drilled into me. I forced myself to hold her gaze.

"Yeah, now that you mention it."

Cailleach shook her head sadly. "You're acting as if you've a choice in the matter when—"

"I do have a choice," I cut in. "I can go to Underhill with Blake."

"Do not put him in that position." The goddess's voice was soft, but steel sat beneath it.

"What position might that be? He didn't want me to leave in the first place."

Cailleach reached across the table and captured one of my hands. "He may not have wanted you to leave, but he understood the wisdom in you going. Did you ever wonder why he didn't argue harder for you to remain?"

My mind tracked backward, plucking details of our conversations before I'd departed from Underhill. We'd been on the same page, I'd thought. Neither of us wanted to be apart, but we recognized how critical it was to fast-track my learning curve, and—

I scrunched my eyes shut to clear my mind. We were getting off base, or I was. "That was then," I said. "This is now. Where am I slated to go next?"

"The simplest solution is Caer Sidi."

My eyebrows shot up. My mouth fell open. I shut it with a snap. Fucking great. Arianrhod's private world. The place she controlled the movements of the moon and the tides.

"Why there?"

"Simple. No one can come or go without Arianrhod's express permission."

My spine straightened. "I'll be her prisoner?"

Cailleach let go of me and slammed the flat of her hand on the table, making the dishes rattle. "You will be her student. Hers and Ceridwen's. 'Tis an honor, not a jail sentence."

Alrighty then. I'd used up all the rope I'd been allotted.

No reason to hang myself. "Do you know for how long?" I mumbled.

"Depends on you and your progress."

I put a few more morsels into my mouth, but my appetite had fled. I was leaving. My respite these past few days had been just that: a postponement, not a reprieve.

No more reason to tarry. I stood and said, "I'll get my things."

Five minutes later, I was back in the library, valise straps slung over one shoulder. "When will I see you again?" I asked.

"I do not know, child. You are destined for far more than I have been shown. I believe our paths will cross, but I am not certain when or how." Cailleach flowed to her feet. The folds of her magic encompassed me. I'd miss her and her steadfast attentiveness.

There it was again. The whole Fate thing. I started to thank her, remembered I already had, and stood tall, shoulders back. I'd done more whining than I was comfortable with. Now was a time to suck it up and press forward. I blanked out my mind, forcing it to a place of stillness. Time would pass. I'd get through this next part.

Whatever it encompassed. However much it took out of me.

Bad attitude, sweetie. Snap out of it. One of my more strident inner voices stepped to the plate.

I stifled a grimace. As usual, my instincts were spot on.

The library turned into a vortex, swirling around me. When it vanished, my consciousness departed too and not in a dreamy, sinking way. Of course not. My head felt like it was exploding from the inside out. My guts warped into a knot. All my muscles burned with an inner fire. When I finally passed out, it was both blessing and relief.

And the last opportunity to not calibrate my every thought, emotion, or action for a good long time.

CHAPTER 3
BLAKE

"You're taking her where?" I screeched at Cailleach before I reined myself in and muttered, "Sorry." The apology stood for all of five seconds before I ruined it when I chucked, "Why wasn't I consulted," into the mix.

Instead of answering, the witch goddess looked askance at me and asked, "What do you have against Caer Sidi?" before adding, "You agreed to Abria's further training with the Celts. You even tracked them down for me."

"Nothing against Arianrhod's home world *per se*, except I can't..." Words faltered. I'd been about to say I couldn't break in, but it would blow my cover and reveal I had tried to do exactly that. The natural world belongs to my people, the Sidhe. We've always resented poaching on the part of the Celts.

Arianrhod squats over her queendom like a dragon guarding her hoard. To her way of thinking, the moon and tide cycles are hers. We see it differently. I've tried to talk with her about it. You can imagine how well those conversations went—before they devolved into geysers of magic, hissing, spitting, and volleys of unkind words.

When it became apparent talking was a dead end, a band of other Daione Sidhe and I took matters into our own hands. We tried to storm the fortress—multiple times. Even the force of our combined magic proved insufficient. Not only couldn't we get in, Arianrhod either moved Caer Sidi or swathed it in enough illusions we couldn't even find it after a while.

I felt the weight of Cailleach's odd, almost colorless gaze. She was waiting to see which way the wind would blow. I could pull rank, maybe, demand Abria return to Underhill, but I'd be on a slippery slope. Abria is my intended, but she's not Sidhe. If I'd formalized our mating bond before her training began, I'd have more of a leg to stand on.

"Why any change of venue at all?" I switched tactics.

The sea witch narrowed her eyes. "We covered that ground before you located the Celts. Did you have more than one teacher?"

Ouch. I batted a hand her way. "Not the point. Most of us come into our skills when we're young."

Cailleach nodded. "Which makes our current endeavor that much more challenging. Abria is far from a lass. She's quite set in her ways." Breath rustled from between Cailleach's thin lips. "I could have continued with her, but I'm not who created her. The Celts have a better grasp of what she's capable of. They're her logical next step."

"Aye, I already agreed with that part. But why Caer Sidi?"

She raked me from head to toe with a knowing look that made me squirm. "It was the safest spot any of us could come up with. No one has breached its borders—not even you."

Heat crept upward from my neck. So much for what I'd hoped was a well-guarded secret. After our last attempt on Caer Sidi, our small band had sworn an oath of silence. We don't like to fail, and we certainly wouldn't have spread it around.

"How do you know about that?" I demanded, ready to excoriate who'd spilled the beans.

A slight shrug. "I have my ways."

Hard to argue with the safety factor—and I did want Abria to be safe. But I also wanted to visit her from time to time. Not a likely occurrence under the circumstances. "How long do you anticipate she'll be there?"

Another shrug. "Depends on her, wouldn't you say? Arianrhod is strict but not unreasonable."

I screwed my mouth into a frown. Not exactly how I'd describe the goddess. I'd tried to reason with her and failed.

"May I see her before she leaves your realm?"

"We had a feeling you'd request as much. She's already gone."

My right hand balled into a fist before I remembered myself and released it. Punching Cailleach would be downright satisfying, but alienating her was the wrong thing to do.

"Since I had no input about her destination, why tell me

at all?" I snarled. Even though I'd smothered my desire to inflict physical violence, I was still furious, and it bled through all over the place.

"She will be your mate. You have a right to know her whereabouts."

Nice of you, my inner voice snarked. For once, I didn't give a crap if Cailleach was monitoring my thoughts.

"Beyond 'knowing her whereabouts,' will I also have leave to visit?"

"That's between you and Arianrhod."

Power thickened, swirling around me. Before I could ask anything else, Cailleach vanished in a haze of silver-blue sparks. The salt smell of the sea lingered in my rooms. I could have gone after her, tried to wring more details out of the witch, but one of the tenets of wisdom is quitting when you're ahead.

In this case, I wasn't exactly ahead, but I hadn't totally embarrassed myself by being an arrogant, entitled dick, either.

I strode to my study, which also serves as a library, determined to see if anything new had shown up in the lore about Caer Sidi. Books and scrolls plopped off the shelves landing in untidy piles on my long reading table. Clouds of dust rose. No excuse for my slovenly housekeeping. I could have set magic to do things for me, but it had always seemed like a waste of good enchantment.

After culling and sorting and stacking, I drew back. What was I thinking? That I'd somehow discover a back way into Caer Sidi. Even if I was successful, which I doubted, what would I do once I got there?

Since Cailleach knew about my past attempts, Arianrhod must as well. We'd had words, none of them pleasant, about other topics—like her grabbing control of the moon and tides. She'd be incensed if I showed up unannounced, and she might take it out on Abria. This wasn't a time for stealth. No. I'd present myself at the front gates—assuming I could locate them—and ask to visit my intended. I didn't see how Arianrhod could possibly say no.

As an aside, she has an interesting, and rather checkered, past. She's always touted herself as the virgin huntress. The huntress part is correct. I've never seen her without a quiver of silver and golden arrows strapped across her back and her bow close to hand. The virgin part is another story. Not that I have firsthand knowledge, but rumors have flown thick and fast about a particular black dragon she had a long-standing affair with. And then there was a Celtic seer, supposedly the love of her life, who traveled far back in time to the beginnings of the British Isles.

She may have gone with him, but didn't remain. I occasionally wondered if he knew about her dragon lover. Or maybe none of the tales were true. Immortality is its own brand of curse. Gossip helps pass the time.

I shooed the books and scrolls back to their places and raised my mind voice to call Abria. She didn't answer. I hadn't expected her to, but it gave me a solid reason to seek her out.

"Not too soon," rolled across my mind.

My head snapped up. Damn it. That was Cailleach. Power bubbled from me, enchantment set to disable any and all spells in the vicinity. Sure enough, her distinctive form shimmered into view.

"I thought you left," I groused.

"Because I wanted you to," she agreed in saccharine tones.

"Why trick me?"

She glided across the room and settled into a chair across from me. "Not a trick so much as breathing space. Sometimes no words will improve a situation, so I waited to see what you'd do."

I angled my head to one side. "And if I'd gone after her?"

"I'd have tried to stop you. Abria just arrived at Caer Sidi. The journey wasn't an easy one, and—"

"How do you know?" I broke in, frantic with worry.

"Because I was there, and it wasn't easy for me." She crooked a finger. "Come along."

"Where are we going?"

The edges of her mouth curved into the closest she ever came to smiling. "Humor an old woman, Sidhe. Besides, so little in your life is a surprise, you might choose to value this one."

I opened my mouth to say I wasn't in the mood for surprises. What came out of it was, "Yes."

"You did that," I accused her.

"I may have." She got to her feet. The same sea-scented power wafted around her, and the walls of my study swirled to darkness.

It's rare that I cede control—to anyone. Who knows why I did this time? Water closed over my head, and I switched to sea-breathing. Schools of small, iridescent fish swam this way and that. A red-mottled octopus with tentacles at least a meter long flitted by. The fish scattered, but not before he (she?) made a meal out of several. After a time, walls made of black and pink coral formed in the depths of the sea. Lights flickered from within casting a warm golden glow to light our path. Sometimes, I'm certain I've been everywhere, yet a place I'd never seen before spread below us.

Excitement rolled through me. There are so few new places, I wanted to savor everything about this one.

"That's the spirit." Cailleach's approval warmed me. My earlier anger faded to fumes.

"What is this place?"

She whipped around, funneling water into a mini-vortex. As she rearranged the sea to do her bidding, she changed. More witch, less human until there was nothing left of her earthly guise. With eyes shading to silver and her hair turning violet, she looked more queen than witch. The planes in her face grew pronounced; beauty lived within her. Not the soft loveliness of a maiden, but the harsh, stern, not-to-be-trifled-with splendor of someone who's lived a long time and expects instant obedience.

"Takes one to know one," I mumbled under my breath. I hadn't forgotten my question, but I no longer expected her to answer it.

Seals swam from the palace, some gray, some brown, some black. Forming a circle, they bowed to Cailleach.

Not seals, Selkies.

This was becoming more and more curious. What possible relationship could she have with the seaweres? They barely talked with anyone outside their ranks, yet this bunch were bent double bowing and scraping before Cailleach.

After beckoning to me, she swam toward the castle. I could have set my own spell in motion and left. After all, I had to worm my way into Arianrhod's good graces, or years might pass with nary a glimpse of Abria.

The Selkies cut through the water with fins and flippers, following the witch goddess. After a measured pause, I brought up the rear. I wouldn't remain long, but the need to know what manner of being Cailleach truly was beat a tattoo through my veins.

Bullshit. She'd ensorcelled me, probably to keep me away from Caer Sidi until the dust settled more. I resented being manipulated, but not enough to pull the plug. Something was afoot. I was part of it—I felt the draw of power not of my own making. It intensified as I swam beneath shimmering lintels and into the castle.

I should have been more cautious, should have been a lot of things, but twenty-twenty hindsight is always crystal clear.

CHAPTER 4
BLAKE

I stood atop a rocky crag watching a battle unfold below. The troops garbed in black and gold were mine. Our enemy wore shades of gray. Smoke rose from piles of bodies. Dragons soared overhead, adding more fire as needed to incinerate the corpses. Every once in a while, a shower of sparks from one dragon or another danced around me.

I hadn't commanded an army this large for centuries. Dropping into the well-timed dance of battle strategies was heady, so intoxicating it absorbed my full attention. Rather like a modern video game, except this was real.

Or was it?

I shook my head to clear my thoughts. Every time I considered anything beyond my role as commander, doubt filled me. Another burst of dragon sparks circled my perch. Several embers landed on my shoulders, and the tension flooding my body retreated. Before, I'd let it go. Not this time. Complacency held me here; it wasn't my friend.

After wrenching my gaze from the hypnotic thrust and parry playing out a few meters below on a rutted green that reminded me of Scotland, I struggled to focus on my situation. How long had I been here? Since it was the only thing I remembered, it had to be a while.

How could this be the sum total of my life? Who was I? More pertinently, who had I been before I stood on this promontory directing a battle?

The answer was so long coming, it shocked me out of my mental fugue. My name, long hidden from common view, is Elwyn Cardassier. The name I've used in recent times is Blake Townsend, Earl of Galloway. I'm Daoine Sidhe, a prince and leader of my people. The information tried to fritter away, but I held it front and center.

Once I remembered myself, everything else came rushing back. None of this was right. I was supposed to be deep in an unknown ocean in Cailleach's stronghold. Curiosity had drawn me there, but my memory of events once I'd swum into the castle wasn't readily accessible. Searing pain jabbed my right temple before forming a band that tightened mercilessly around my head. My vision shattered into bits and pieces, no longer forming a cohesive whole.

Fuck!

I grabbed the sides of my head and funneled a cool stream of watery magic to counteract the pain. Since I'd stopped paying attention, my troops shifted from winning to running for their lives.

"Nooooo!" I shouted. "Return to your posts now, you sorry bunch of rotters."

But then I stepped back. I could use magic—a whole pig-pile of it—to force my men back into position, but I was done. I no longer cared about winning or anything beyond freeing myself.

Someone—probably the sea witch in cahoots with the Celts—had laid a cunning, velvet-lined snare. How had I been so easily fooled? How could I have forgotten Abria and the rest of the Sidhe? I'd already failed my people once by extended absences from my post as their regent. How in the hell long had I been gone this time?

All good questions. Could I remain present, focus long enough to extricate myself? My troops were fleeing once more. I let them go. Once they reached the edge of the battlefield, they vanished.

I blinked stupidly at the place they'd occupied seconds before. Crap. This was getting worse and worse.

"Illusion. The whole thing was naught but illusion," I muttered through clenched teeth. I was slipping—and rather badly—to have let this charade go on as long as it had.

Aye, and I wanted to know exactly how long that had been, but I wouldn't find answers here. Before Cailleach or anyone else could show up to taunt me— or worse, try to push me back under their thumb—I funneled power into a journey spell aimed for Underhill. I'd say my mea culpas to my people, figure out how long I'd been stuck with my head up my ass, and then storm Caer Sidi's gates.

I had no doubt Arianrhod was joined at the hip with

Cailleach, and maybe Ceridwen as well. They'd set wheels in play guaranteeing I wouldn't interfere with the next phase of Abria's training.

And I'd walked right into their web, a willing participant to their meddling. Sidhe sit damned close to the top of the magical pyramid. We command more power than anyone except the Celts—and apparently, Cailleach.

My spell was slow to ignite. When my surroundings didn't vanish like they should have, I poured enchantment into my escape hatch. If I didn't break free now, who knew when I'd have another chance. Being held against my will broke every covenant that binds magic wielders.

"Yeah, I'll be sure to mention that next time I see one of you bitches," I growled determined there would never, never be a next time. Big words since our paths would cross again. Whether I held the sorceresses to task for kidnapping me remained to be seen.

Nothing changed, but no one popped up to stop me, either, so I backpedaled and sorted through each element in my spell, experimenting with more fire, more air, and more water. The last one did the trick. Liquid cascaded around me, drenching me. It was poor form. The elements are supposed to remain in my mind, but I was desperate.

Finally, finally, the place I'd been standing for goddess only knew how long shimmered to nothing, leaving me suspended in darkness. Trading water for a firmly held vision of Underhill, I pushed until the link that binds all Sidhe to our home snagged my magic.

Relief spilled through me, but I couldn't afford to relax. Not yet. I was vulnerable in the in-between place. It's why we spend as little time here as possible. Journey spells are as quick and clean and neat as we can make them.

I'd aimed for my chamber in Underhill. I ended up in one of the lower tunnels near our main meeting room. Not quite believing I'd made good on my escape, I grabbed handfuls of dirt and inhaled deeply. Anyone with strong magic could craft an illusion of Underhill, but they'd never be able to mirror its unique fragrance.

The scents of wildflowers, damp stones, and wet evergreens slammed into my brain. Yes! I truly was home. More shaken than I was willing to admit, I remained crouched next to a curved wall. It wasn't very dignified, but I didn't care.

"Where in the goddess's name have you been?" A familiar voice and footsteps hustled toward me.

I straightened and walked toward Kirwan's voice.

"You didn't answer me." He strode into view, moving far quicker than was his norm. He's one of the few Sidhe who don't employ spells to stave off the aging process. A black silk robe hung off thin shoulders. White hair grew in a circle around a large bald spot. Wrinkles sat atop other wrinkles, lending him the appearance of an aged shaman.

"Because I have no good reply." I rolled my tired shoulders back and stood as straight as I could manage.

"Everyone's been worried," Kirwan went on. "Most of us, anyway. A few are convinced your speech about being here more of the time was just a bunch of pretty words."

I hesitated, but not for long. The truth would serve me better than lies. Never mind it would cast me in an unfavorable light and reveal I'd been duped. "Follow me," I invited. "I'd like a cup of mead, and then I'll tell you everything."

Bushy white brows shot up.

"Aye, everything," I repeated myself. "I made a rather serious mistake, and it cost me. How long have I been gone?"

His brows edged up another notch. "You don't know?"

"If I did, I wouldn't have asked."

"Going on two months."

Breath rattled from my lungs. This could have been so much worse. Like two years. Or two centuries. I walked toward our council chamber with Kirwan by my side. Once we were within and I'd poured generous jots of mead into crystal goblets, I said, "Drop a truth net over me, please."

Surprise radiated from the old mage, but he complied. Once the net clanked into place around me, I started at the beginning. I'd thought it would be difficult to reveal my fall from grace, my stupidity at being conned, but the words came easily once I began talking.

CHAPTER 5
ABRIA

Good thing Cailleach and Birgit taught me to cloak my thoughts. Remaining warded turned into a perennial state in Caer Sidi. Arianrhod's world was intriguing and strange. Violet skies sported pale-blue clouds, and the temperature was always the same: cool but not overly cold. The empty countryside was filled with lush shrubbery, lakes, and unusual trees with silvery boles. They whispered my name as I walked among them. In their arboreal way, they made me feel more welcome than Arianrhod did.

Much like Underhill, Caer Sidi perched at a nexus that touched Earth and several other worlds. From what I'd been able to ascertain, no one but Arianrhod actually lived here. And now me, of course, but I was counting the days until I could courteously bid her farewell.

I rolled my mental eyes, hoping to hell I could manage courteous. The goddess was cool to the point of being chilly.

Cailleach hadn't always been pleased with my efforts, but the witch goddess cared about me. It was why she'd volunteered to take me under her wing in the first place.

Arianrhod not only didn't care, she made it clear I was burdensome from the moment I arrived. Not a task she would have willingly taken on were it not for pressure from Ceridwen and goddess only knew who else. I hadn't been in that great a shape when I plummeted out of my journey spell and into Caer Sidi. It was a rough transit. I could have used a meal and a few hours' rest. Instead, we dove into a training session so intense it left me with a punishing headache and my guts twisted into a hard, painful knot.

I toughed it out—and withstood a burning temptation to tell her to go fuck herself. I've been here for a couple of months now. Far from settling in, developing a comfort zone, nothing's changed. I get up, eat, train most of the day, eat again, and sleep. All my meals are by myself. Much of my training is as well. Arianrhod outlines the task du jour and then leaves. Mostly, she never bothers to check how well I mastered the material.

The next day, we move to something new. I've tried asking questions about how certain elements fit together, but she never answers me.

I wouldn't have guessed both the moon and tides had guardians, protectors who reported to her. They showed up every morning and night like clockwork, but then they left. Soon after I arrived, I asked how such an unusual situation had developed since she'd taken credit for the moon and tides for as long as my memory extended.

She told me to mind my own business and worry about developing my magic.

Alrighty, then. No warm, fuzzy personal relationship with this goddess. Like I already said, I ate alone, slept in a tiny chamber high in her castle, and only saw her during the start of training sessions.

I've always been self-sufficient, probably because of my bond with animals. None of them lived in this world, not so much as a bird or an insect. At least, I didn't believe they did. They'd have sought me out quick enough, and it never happened.

Early on in my tenure, I started keeping track of days the old-fashioned way by scribing subtle marks in an unobtrusive spot on the wall behind my bed. No writing materials here. Certainly no electronics. Like all magical worlds, they probably wouldn't work here, anyway.

"Abria!" The goddess's voice held a sharp note suggesting it wasn't the first time she'd spoken my name.

I lowered my hands from the pattern I'd been painting in the air and turned to face her. Usually, I kept my gaze downcast, but I was sick of presenting a subservient demeanor.

"Yes?" I stared her down. Not the easiest task. Her eyes, one silver and the other gold, had an unpleasant way of boring into my soul. I came within a hairsbreadth of asking why she was even here. I'd seen her hours ago and hadn't planned on another sighting until the following day.

She scrunched her pale brows into a thick line. "What were you daydreaming about?"

The question took me by surprise since it was the first personal question she'd asked since my arrival.

"Nothing important," I muttered. Telling her how miserable I was in her special realm wouldn't buy me shit.

"Pfft. Aye, that goes without saying, but you didn't answer my question."

I bristled. How dare she dismiss my thoughts without even knowing what they were? I've always been quick to anger; my temper has never been my friend. Before it roared to life, I squashed it.

Hoping a half-truth would fit the bill, and get her off my case, I said, "This experience is...different from my years with Cailleach. I'm hoping we'll come to appreciate one another, and—"

"Appreciate?" she broke in, a snort almost obliterating the word. "What could I possibly find to appreciate in you? We made you. Had plans for you. Every time I lay eyes on you, our mistakes leap out at me."

The anger I'd controlled threatened to break its bonds. Hot words strutted in the back of my throat, choking me. I wanted to yell at her, make her understand I hadn't done all that badly considering she and Ceridwen and the Morrigan had abandoned me.

Applying a great deal of effort, I made myself examine her words. They were the key to why she spent as little time as possible in my presence.

"I'm not unhappy with myself," I told her.

"But you could have been so much more. It's why I volunteered to teach you, except you throw that gift back in my lap every day." She folded her arms under her breasts. "The same way you kicked sand in our faces when you vanished from the cell where we'd placed you."

My tattered temper sputtered to life. "Did you hear yourself?" I demanded. "You called my home a cell. And it was. When the animals helped me escape, I was glad, glad I tell you. I looked over my shoulder for centuries expecting one of you to come after me. Except you never did."

Still raging, I stamped my foot. It was juvenile, but I was beyond caring. "I was delighted none of you cared enough to look for me. You didn't give me anything when I was under your noses. The best gift was your indifference. I treasured it."

Stop there, an inner voice thundered through my mind. I wasn't so far gone I didn't listen to it.

Breathing hard, I waited for the goddess to slay me on the spot, or whatever goddesses did to miscreants who had the nerve to talk back.

She angled her head to one side, holding me firmly in her gaze. "We did talk about it, about going after you. Most of us were opposed. A few, Ceridwen, the Morrigan, and me, argued your cause."

I considered mumbling, "Thanks," but didn't. Them not coming after me was far more of a favor than she knew.

Instead, I asked, "Why the interest? You didn't do anything for me while I remained in my 'cell.'"

"You don't remember, but we arranged it so you wouldn't." She crooked a finger my way and turned before walking out of the hall where we trained. Crystal windows lined one wall, offering a faux view of a mountainous land-scape. Soothing to stare at, but nothing in Caer Sidi looked anything like it.

I glared at her retreating form. She clearly wanted me to

follow her, but I was of two minds. Part of me had grown used to solitude. I wasn't at all certain I wanted a closer relationship with one of the three who'd masterminded my existence.

What would happen if I went back to my practice session? Would anything change? I raised my hands and began resurrecting my casting before dropping them to my sides and following Arianrhod's footsteps. I'd be a fool to ignore an opportunity to hear her out...

She hadn't exactly said she'd talk with me, but if she didn't, I hadn't lost anything.

"Nothing ventured, nothing gained," I mumbled half aloud.

Corridors branched this way and that. I hadn't spent much time exploring the castle beyond the places where I trained, ate, and slept. In my own way, I'd been as withdrawn as the goddess.

Figuring out where she'd gone was simple. Power spilled from her leaving a shining path that glittered enticingly. My journey ended in a grand chamber I hadn't seen before. Another row of crystal windows yielded the same view as the one in my practice arena. Impossible since these windows faced in the opposite direction.

But then, I'd known the scene was fake.

A fire crackled at the far end of the room. Beyond thick rugs embossed with myriad battle scenes, the cavernous chamber was devoid of furnishings. Arianrhod sat cross-legged on the floor near a stone hearth. She'd removed her ever-present bow and quiver of golden arrows and laid them next to her.

"Took you long enough," she observed.

I didn't have the energy or inclination to spar with her. "What do you want from me?" I demanded and strode toward her until I was only about a meter away. The warmth from the fire was welcome; I held out my hands.

She patted the carpet. I didn't sit next to her but did drop into a crouch with my fingertips still extended to the crackling warmth of the blaze. It had to be fueled by magic. From what I could determine, no trees grew here that weren't sentient, and they would have thrown nine kinds of fits if any of their kinfolk had been chopped down.

"A better question," she murmured, "is what you want from me. You agreed to this arrangement, to coming here."

"Didn't think I had a choice."

Arianrhod shook her head. "We may not be getting along especially well, but at least so far we've been honest with one another."

I pulled my hands back and used them to stabilize my position. "I was honest. Choice is relative. Cailleach intimated I had a major role to play in something bearing down on us. She made it abundantly clear I needed more than she'd taught me to hold up my end."

The goddess angled her head to one side. "Did she provide details about the upcoming crisis?"

"No. I hoped you would do that."

"Mmph."

Tossing caution aside, I asked, "What does that mean?" She wouldn't answer if she didn't want to, but I was done pussyfooting around. If she booted me out of Caer Sidi, so be it. I missed Blake, and so far I hadn't learned anything here he couldn't have taught me.

A flare of brilliant white receded. In its wake sat a tray with a silver teapot, two mugs, and an assortment of tea cakes. "Help yourself." Arianrhod flapped a hand my way.

I didn't see any reason not to, so I poured myself a cup of fragrant tea that smelled of jasmine and roses. The cakes were buttery delights with layers of jam tucked between crumbly sheets of pastry. I ate the two I'd taken and then snatched two more. My fare here, foraged from the kitchens, had been far more pedestrian.

"Is there a cook in residence?"

"Pfft." Arianrhod trapped me between her golden eye and her silver one. "Have you seen any kitchen staff?"

I shook my head. Feeling bold, I took a stab at answering her question. "You asked what I want from you." At her nod, I continued. "I hoped when I was done here, my formal training would be over, and I could get on with my mystery task."

"Watch what you wish for." She waggled a finger in my direction and stretched toward the tea tray, securing provisions for herself.

I shrugged my shoulders. "How bad could it be?" I blurted. "I've been on my own since I escaped from the Celtic stronghold. Somehow, I've managed, and—"

"That was a different world. Many elements have shifted."

I set my cup down on the rug. Its weave muted the *thunk* the ceramic would have made if I'd plunked it on a bare floor. When I'd started my journey with Cailleach and Birgit,

I'd known so little, everything I added to my arsenal was a plus. That was no longer the case. This was rubber-meets-road time. No more running blind. In the absence of answers, I'd return to Underhill and figure things out on the fly.

"Vague doesn't cut it for me. Not anymore. I need information, details. It's one thing to train, but I'm training in a vacuum. I have no idea which of the skills I'm developing will be useful since I don't know what's coming."

"And that matters, why?"

Her question caught me by surprise. "It just does," I sputtered. "I'm not a youth any longer. All of you are treating me like I have no common sense, as if I can't be trusted with classified information when the subject at hand is me."

"Did it occur to you we're shielding you?" She drew her fair brows together.

"Even if you are, I don't want your protection."

Arianrhod laid her mug aside and dusted shortbread crumbs off her fingers. "Remember," she admonished, "you asked for this. Once heard, there's no going back."

A shiver started at the base of my neck and crept down my spine. I shook it off. No matter what she had to say, how horrible could it be? I'd faced demons and monsters. There were limits to the bad things inhabiting the world.

"When we began the process that produced you," she began, "we had no idea how long it would take. Ceridwen consulted her cauldron to home in on an auspicious time, and if we'd completed our task quicker..."

She closed her teeth over her lower lip before continuing. "The, erm, process was far more complicated than we anticipated, mostly because disagreements rose amongst us. Many of them. What should have taken weeks, required years."

Twin vertical lines formed between her brows. "You'd no sooner been created than Ceridwen raced into our hidden workshop shrieking dire predictions. We'd waited too long. The stars were out of line with our efforts."

"What about the moon and the tides?" I snarked before mumbling, "Never mind."

My off-the-cuff comment earned me a pained look. "You were already here, having grown from babe to youngster, when Ceridwen warned us." The goddess shook her head. "We couldn't unmake you, and because we couldn't agree on what to do next, we sequestered you in a spot we were certain would be safe. Years passed, but you—"

"Stop," I broke in. "You're not telling me anything I don't already know. The piece you're waltzing around is the content of Ceridwen's 'dire predictions.'"

"They were only prophecies," Arianrhod protested. "No one was certain they'd come to fruition."

"You were certain enough to stuff me in a cell."

The goddess winced. "When did your use of language turn so plainspoken, child?"

Her question was rhetorical; I didn't bother answering it, just stared at her waiting for clarification.

A sigh burbled through her lips. She passed fingertips over her discarded bow and quiver of arrows as if they'd somehow help. "The timing of your creation coincided with an alteration in the ley lines feeding power to both our

Celtic realm as well as Earth. It was serious enough, we decided to move on, leave Earth behind."

"Coincided?" I tipped my head to one side. If there was one thing I did not believe in, it was coincidences.

She cleared her throat, poured more tea, and drank deep. "We may have borrowed power from the lines to create you. At the time, we had no idea they wouldn't be able to regenerate the slack." Another pause before she added, "We weren't the only ones who noticed the shift. Every magic wielder was aware of it since they had to modify how they manipulated the elements to form spells.

"Many blamed us—another reason to leave. Some suspected it had to run deeper than a Celtic mishap, so bands of sorcerers hunted for the source of the disturbance."

"Since my birth, or whatever it was?" I interrupted.

Arianrhod nodded. "Aye, since we created you."

I tucked my legs under my butt and sat straighter. "What a bunch of blundering fools if they've been looking all this time."

"'Tisn't entirely on them. Our spells protected you, they still are, but as your power has grown, our ability to shield you has lessened. Once you fully claim the sum total of your magic, you'll be visible to your enemies."

My mouth went dry; swallowing became difficult. Why in the hell hadn't someone decided I had a right to that tidbit of data? "Does Blake know?" I croaked.

"Nay. We didn't tell him. If we had, he'd never have left your side."

Okay, then. Moving on. "Were you ever going to tell me?"

"We were waiting for you to ask."

Something about her tone galled me. "What if I hadn't?" I pressed, curious what she'd say. This whole mess had turned into a surreal experience, one where I was on the outside looking in on someone else's life. Except the life in question belonged to me.

"Not sure." A slight shrug. "But you did, so it's a moot point."

I unclenched my jaw. "Who's hunting me?"

"Who isn't? Whoever finds you and sacrifices you will set the ley lines right again. They haven't supported strong magic since your birth."

The sick feeling plaguing me shot skyward. "Is that true?" I gritted. "The part about sacrificing me fixing everything?"

"No one knows, child. I suspect not, but these beliefs are like urban myths. They develop a life of their own."

"With mine on the chopping block." I slammed a fist into the carpet, ignoring pain ratcheting along my knuckles and up my arm.

"Stop feeling sorry for yourself. Nothing has changed, Abria, except your knowledge. What you haven't asked is why we're training you."

"Cailleach said I had a key role to play." My tone was dull. Far from rising to the occasion, I wanted off this choo-choo.

"You do," she said brightly. "Your task, once your power has fully developed, is to set the ley lines right. If you manage it, those who are hunting you will back off. At least, we hope they will. Some quests aren't so easily dissuaded."

I stumbled to my feet. Sitting still wasn't working for me. "How do I even find these ley lines?" I asked.

"You can't. Not yet. Once your skills have improved, your path will become clear."

"You hope," I muttered and loped from the room. She didn't call after me, but I hadn't expected her to.

Sitting in my room stewing over being a cosmic pawn was self-indulgent. Instead, I pelted down one hallway after another until I found a door leading outside. Wrapped in the velvet of dusk, I opened my heart to the trees. They sang to me, crooned lullabies, until I walked into a grove where they surrounded me with clean, pure love.

Not one had ulterior motives. Their lack of an agenda was refreshing.

Exhausted and distrustful of everyone who'd had a hand in making me a target, I wrapped my arms around a large, silvery tree bole and hung on. It took a long while before all the tension leached out of me.

It would take even longer before I ever trusted anyone again.

I have no idea how long I stood there before soft hooting drew my attention skyward. An enormous golden owl floated above, wings spread to ride the air currents.

Shock cascaded through me. Joy followed. The owl was the first creature I'd seen here. Its presence went a long way toward filling the emptiness inside me. I let go of the tree, thanking it lavishly for its care, and slid between two thick trunks into a clearing.

The owl perched on a bush, golden eyes fixed on me. My vow to never trust again evaporated. I held out an arm; the owl flew to me, talons digging deep where he gripped my forearm. He clacked his beak while I smoothed wing feathers into place.

"How are you here?" I asked. *"Does Arianrhod know?"*

Another beak clack. *"Aye. She thought you needed a friend."*

Oh-oh... Extending magic, I touched the owl lightly, testing for whether it was real or merely an artifact designed to keep me quiescent. Fat, dumb, and happy to coin a modern saying. My examination was over in seconds. Fascinating. The bird was not only real, but brimming with magic. Only some of the animals who seek me out are magical.

Unicorns, for example.

"Stop that," the owl squawked.

Apparently, I'd hit a sensitive spot with my unicorn visualization, or maybe my cursory examination had been uncomfortable.

"Sorry." I hesitated, searching for words but not finding any. I'd sound like a whining idiot if I launched into a diatribe chronicling my problems. It wasn't as if Arianrhod beat or starved me. Perhaps she'd sensed her inability to provide emotional support and scared up the owl to fill in.

Regardless, I was thrilled he was here.

"Want to hunt?" Without waiting for an answer, he leapt from my arm and winged northward.

I loped after him, my heart lighter than it had been since leaving Cailleach's lair.

CHAPTER 6
BLAKE

Kirwan didn't cluck over me; neither did he chide me for being drawn in. The spell hadn't imprisoned me. Not exactly. Crafty use of illusion had diverted me from my purpose and served as a reminder why we'd never trusted the Celts.

He helped me convene an impromptu council gathering. Once I'd provided an expurgated version to explain my absence and not make myself appear a total fool, I parceled out tasks and returned to my chamber to prepare for a journey to Caer Sidi.

Presumably, Abria was still in residence there. If she wasn't, I'd hunt down Cailleach.

"Are you certain you don't want one of us to accompany you?" Kirwan asked for the tenth time.

The question rankled; beneath it lay the implicit intimation I wasn't capable of watching out for myself. Maybe I was overreacting, still raw from my stint playing Warcraft. It was one thing for me to doubt myself, quite another for my subjects to have reservations about my abilities.

I shooed Kirwan out of my chambers. I had to pull my head out of my ass and get on with things. Abria's place was next to me. Far as I was concerned, her training at the hands of strangers was over. I'd provide what she needed next, or, if I couldn't, I'd locate someone appropriate to the task.

Watch it, I cautioned myself. If she didn't see things the same way, forcing her away from Arianrhod—if I even could —wasn't the swiftest idea. She'd resent me for sticking my oar into the mix. And Arianrhod might call down the wrath of her kinsmen. The last place I wanted it to land was on the Sidhe, mages I was sworn to protect.

I tossed items into a rucksack: a warm coat, a few biscuits since I hadn't taken time to eat. No powders, potions, or enchanted stones. I've never relied on magical accoutrements. If I couldn't get into Caer Sidi via straightforward measures, I'd figure something else out.

Aye, like what?

I ground my teeth since I lacked a ready answer. Before, I'd been prepared to storm the fortress via any means available to me. I halted my preparations and sucked in a steadying breath followed by a few more.

I've always viewed myself as reasonable, approachable. Apparently, that worldview wasn't universally shared. If it had been, some Celtic messenger would have hunted me down and told me to stay away while Abria honed her craft. I shook my head. They'd been so certain of my pushback, they hadn't bothered to even discuss it with me.

Nay, they'd booted me to the curb.

If I hadn't seen through the battleground ruse, how long would they have held me there?

I didn't much care for the answer. They might never have freed me. One of the curses of immortality is a laissez-faire attitude toward time. A hundred years or a thousand merge and become one and the same.

A petty part of me wanted vengeance, to get even, which was idiotic. Sidhe magic is robust, but nothing stacked up against the gods' power. Maybe they'd respect me since I'd wormed my way out of their clutches.

Maybe.

More likely, no one even noticed I was gone. I got a firm grip on my runaway thoughts. Ruminating about any of the time since I'd swum into what I thought was Cailleach's underwater realm was pointless. If Arianrhod opened Caer Sidi's gates to me, my focus had to be on Abria, not on peppering the goddess with "how could you?" questions.

My pride was hurt. So what? Spinning my wheels playing Warcraft was far from the worst thing that had happened to me over the long years of my existence.

I teetered back and forth before dropping a few seeking crystals into my bag, hoping I wouldn't need them to augment my native abilities. Overall, my experience is if I can't get something done the old-fashioned way, adding gizmos to the mix rarely did anything beyond muddying the waters.

Some of my younger kin rely on potions and powders and crystals. There's even the occasional familiar. I always figured it was because their own ability was lacking in some way, but maybe I'd been wrong to turn my back on potential allies.

After chucking amethyst, tourmaline, and a robin's-egg-sized emerald into a pocket, I visualized Rait Castle's side yard and invited a spell to drop me there. Dusk had fallen. Soon it would be dark; days in the northlands are short this time of year.

A fine drizzle misted from above. The unending gray mirrored my bleak mood. I should be elated I'd escaped, that I'd ended my enforced stasis and was on my way to rescue Abria—

Poor choice of words, mate. She might not believe she requires rescuing.

Cursing semantics, I snatched up a stick and drew a power circle in the wet earth, marking each of the four compass points. I'd use it as a beacon to return me to this very spot.

The Celts had duped me once. I wouldn't provide as juicy a target next time.

Fuck. There wouldn't be a next time.

Bold words, and not especially productive ones. I couldn't control the future; all I could manage was my part in it. I shored up my circle and considered how to begin my journey.

Once I'd known how to locate Caer Sidi, but Arianrhod kept moving it. My best bet was to go to its original location and track her from that point. It was quite the longshot since her trail—if she'd left one in the first place—would have grown more than cold.

If the Celts had gone to all the trouble of sucking me into

game-land, surely, they'd taken pains to shield Caer Sidi. Maybe. Cailleach had been forthcoming with Abria's location. And equally clear I was to leave her alone.

My fist closed so hard on the stick I'd been holding, it splintered and broke. No one had monitored—or modulated—my movements since I'd worn short pants. Eh, bad analogy. I'd raced through Underhill buck naked until one of my mentors tossed a robe over my shoulders when I was around ten. I'd liked the feel of the silky garment. When I returned to my chamber, someone had stocked an armoire with trousers, tunics, and a few more robes.

One of many messages the latitude extended to children was over. Everyone understood I'd be saddled with full responsibility for my people; those first few years of idyllic freedom had to end sometime.

I'd been standing in the Rait Castle courtyard, rucksack dangling from one hand for half an hour. What in the goddess's name was wrong with me? My mind kept dashing off in a whole lot of unrelated directions, none of which would help me find Abria. Before something else intervened, I visualized the place I'd last crossed into Caer Sidi, slung my rucksack across my back, and launched a journey spell to take me there.

Underhill vanished handily, but the smooth, peaceful darkness signaling a transit between worlds never materialized. Instead, I ratcheted through a series of tunnels bouncing off the sides courtesy of blasts of icy air.

What in the unholy hell had happened? It couldn't be my casting. I'd just traveled from where I'd been mired playing a Warcraft-esque game. That spell had been slow off the blocks, but once it caught, I'd hit my destination quickly.

Oof! Breath swooshed from me when my shoulder contacted something sharp sticking out of one wall. I could do better than this. My spell should proffer ability to control events not be victimized by them.

Yeah. Right. I hadn't done a bang-up job. So far, the only thing getting banged up was me.

Before a collision took out my other shoulder, I carefully added fire to my working. It's the most powerful element, and one I apply judiciously. This transit had already taken twice as long as it should. Wrestling with my power was demoralizing. It was lethargic, slow to respond.

Were the Celts monitoring my every move? Was that why the passage was brutal?

"Give it up," I growled. The sound of my voice had a steadying effect. With no warning, the wall to my right took on a glittery aspect. Usually, I'd exercise caution, particularly given how rough this trip had been, but I wanted out of the darkness. If I hit the wrong spot, I'd sort things out once I was free.

Sure enough, the glittery place formed a gateway. I barreled through raising defensive magic as I went. Ready for anything from demons to griffons to trolls, I spun in a wide arc hunting for enemies. Wind hit me full in the face. Bracing and laced with the briny smell of the ocean, it reassured me I hadn't missed the mark entirely.

Still on Earth, I stood on a rocky, deserted promontory at the southern tip of South Island, New Zealand. On this side of the world, it was morning. Gulls screeched overhead;

waves crashed on rocks, withdrew, and rolled forward once more.

So far, so good.

But what about how I got here?

I didn't bother answering the part of my brain working overtime. Instead, I hunted for landmarks. One boulder—the erstwhile gateway to Caer Sidi—was unique. It looked like a lazy, reclining walrus. I couldn't see it, so I built a distinctive cairn to mark my starting point and hurried up the beach. If I didn't locate it in a reasonable amount of time, I'd return and explore the other way.

So long as I kept the ocean in sight, I couldn't go wrong.

Or could I?

When my first quarter hour of searching turned up zilch, I added magic to the mix. Mistake. It bounced back and slapped me hard. Switching things up, I cast about for an errant Celt who might have hidden themselves among the tumble of rocks. I came up goose eggs on that one too.

Determined to figure this out, I continued my search first in one direction and then backtracked and tried another. The day was nearly over when I sank into a crouch. The boulder I hunted was unmistakable and huge. No one could have moved it. Only one explanation remained: it was sitting behind a spell. One I couldn't penetrate.

I tried kindling my link with Abria, expecting it to boomerang back and pound me. It didn't. A handsome, tawny owl with golden eyes winged through the fading light. It hadn't been there a moment before. I'd have noticed because it was four times the size of most owls and power shimmered around its wing feathers.

Could it be one of the Celts wearing a different shape?

I girded myself for the creature to swoop down and rake its talons across my exposed face before it morphed into one of the gods, probably Gwydion. If I'd thought deeper, I'd have understood he'd be the last one Arianrhod would seek help from. He'd been instrumental in revealing the sham of her virgin myth by presenting one of her children in front of an audience.

I wasn't thinking about much except evading the owl. Ridiculous since he'd already seen me. Squaring my shoulders, I faced the bird, keeping my gaze glued on him. He dipped his wings from side to side and scribed an arc in the sky before turning westward.

I stared after him. Was this a chance meeting? Unlikely. Not many magical owls, and certainly none on this godforsaken strip of rocky beach extending into the rowdy Southern Ocean.

He turned, dipped a wing, and resumed flying in the same direction. After he repeated the action once more, I got it and traipsed after him. Caution ruled today, or what was left of it. The moment it appeared I was headed for another trap or maze or whatever the Celts had in mind for me this time, I'd exit immediately.

To be on the safe side, I readied a travel spell and held it in abeyance.

The owl circled an empty place at the end of a spit of land three times. The hiss and crackle of magic sputtered around me, and the obelisk I'd been hunting emerged from shadows.

Amid hooting and a few more wing flutters, the owl

disappeared through the gateway I remembered. Was this another trap? Even if it was, I didn't care. If I didn't follow the bird through, the illusion might resurrect itself.

I'd never find Abria then. Not until Arianrhod was good and done with her.

The hissing intensified; the obelisk wavered. It was do it now or kick myself forever. Once I've made up my mind, I rarely second guess my choices. Holding the gateway with magic, I hurried through before it slammed shut in my face.

CHAPTER 7

ABRIA

The next few days were the best I'd passed in Caer Sidi. The owl, Hedrek, became my constant companion. We trained together, and I swear I worked harder because I didn't feel so alone. Odd because I'd spent virtually my entire existence by myself.

With one big difference.

Before, I'd always had the option of a friendly rodent or insect to break my solitude. In Caer Sidi, I'd felt more isolated than anywhere else, and it sucked hope out of me. The owl changed all that. Because I worked harder, I anticipated my tenure in this odd place would draw to a close sooner rather than never.

The goddess and I would never have the relationship I'd had with Cailleach, but she'd been intuitive enough to provide what was missing. I tried to thank her, but she waved it aside. I remembered what she'd disclosed that night in the castle great room, the bit about how looking at me reminded her how badly the Celts had failed.

Talk about two-edged swords. I'd never seen myself as a failure, and it was disconcerting she, and apparently her Celtic cohort, had wished for so much more. It was rather like being a disappointment to critical parents where no matter how much I accomplished it would never be enough.

Hedrek and I fell into a routine. I took to keeping my chamber window open since his preferred hunting time was while I slept, but he was always there in the morning, usually with the remains of something scattered across my tile floor.

"Where do you find game?" I asked that first morning.

"Earth."

I blinked at him before it registered. "You're traveling back and forth."

"Not much choice. Nothing to eat here."

The way he'd hooted it, so matter-of-fact, made me laugh. We talked about many things after that, but he was evasive about where he'd been before Arianrhod had invited him to Caer Sidi.

Or ordered him, although that option seemed remote. The owl was one independent cuss. Arianrhod could order all she liked, but it wouldn't buy her compliance. Not from Hedrek.

I'd probably never know why he agreed except he was drawn to me just like everything with fur and fins and feathers and scales. He might not have disclosed much about himself, but I made up for the both of us. He was a good listener when I told him about Blake and how I'd ended up Arianrhod's prisoner, er guest.

Because of him, I moved past my reluctant recruit phase.

Arianrhod hadn't changed. She assigned new tasks every day without bothering to check my progress on earlier ones. Where Cailleach insisted on perfection, Arianrhod either assumed I absorbed her lessons, or she didn't care what I got out of them.

When the rubber met the road, I'd set out to find the ley lines, do what I could to mend the disturbance, and do my damnedest to escape intact. When I asked if she'd accompany me, she'd given me one of those long, patronizing stares and asked what I thought.

I took it as a no.

I never mentioned my quest to the owl. I was staunchly against putting any animal in harm's way for my sake. Blake would come with me if I gave him any encouragement at all, but I didn't want his death on my conscience, either. Not that he could die, but he could end up trapped in the *Dreaming* for the remainder of eternity.

Dinner had long since passed. Hedrek had left to hunt, and I sat hunched over a musty scroll reviewing what I'd learned the past couple of days. Any ambivalence I'd had about my lessons was gone. I've lived long enough to recognize there'd come a time when I wished I knew more.

My mage light burned blue-white, illuminating the ancient vellum. I'd learned to read any number of arcane languages during my stint with Cailleach. That skill was coming in handy. I reached for what had been a mug of tea only to find it empty.

My eyes ached. Long past time for a break, so I carried the teapot to a spigot in the wall, refilled it, and heated the water with a wisp of a spell. After cleaning out the glob of herbs from the strainer, I added fresh leaves and poured boiling water over them. The room filled with the scents of lavender, anise, and rosemary. As I breathed in hungrily, the sense of peace I craved washed over me in waves.

For the first time in a long while, I believed everything would come out all right. That I'd triumph in the end. A muffled snort burbled from my lips. Wishful thinking? Hubris?

The future would prove me right—or wrong.

Power pulsed, bright and compelling. My head snapped up. Hedrek's essence was part of the mix, but only part. When I sorted the rest of it, I shot to my feet scanning madly for a gateway.

Ha. Could have saved myself time. The owl swooshed through the window like always, but stretched behind him, riding unseen air currents, was Blake. He did a somersault midair and landed in a crouch.

I tackled him, wrapping my arms around his shoulders and inhaling his unique scent. He smelled like a composite of all the good things in the natural world: salty oceans, dripping evergreens, damp granite, lush wildflowers. A brisk peck on the side of my head reminded me Hedrek hovered above us.

"Where'd you find him?" I asked the owl.

Another peck, this one harder. "What? No thank you?" Hedrek hooted.

"I already thanked you, but I'll do it again," Blake

replied. "Without your help, I'd never have located the portal." He rolled us to a sit and hugged me back.

"At least one of you appreciates me." The owl moved up a meter or two and flew large lazy circles around my chamber.

I couldn't imagine Blake, Daoine Sidhe prince, ever having trouble finding his way anywhere. "Thank you very much," I told the owl. "Saved you some nuts. They're on the counter."

Feathers brushed the top of my head as the bird switched directions and curled his talons around the edge of my tiny kitchen counter. This room was small, but it held all the essentials: kitchen, bed, desk, chair, even a cramped bathroom tucked behind a curtain.

With Hedrek occupied eating, I focused my full attention on Blake and laced my fingers into his silky dark hair. Gods but he was gorgeous with his shoulder-length black hair, deep, dark eyes, and a to-die-for body. Broad shoulders topped a lithe build with long legs and slender hips. Full, kissable lips nested atop a square chin. Flared cheekbones lent him an exotic look, almost Middle Eastern.

Impeccably dressed as usual, he wore dark pants, a blue cashmere sweater, and a tweed jacket. Because he hadn't bothered with a glamour —why would he, no humans to shock here—his black wings shimmering with jewel tones were folded against his back.

"Why couldn't you find the entrance?" I demanded, followed by, "What took you so long?"

Oops.

I brushed my lips across his in apology. Diplomacy has never been one of my strong points.

He placed a hand over one of mine and squeezed. "Two very good questions. I couldn't find the portal because it was shrouded in spells I couldn't detect." A sigh rushed past his lips. "And it took me so long because someone—likely the Celts—didn't want me interfering with your lessons."

I frowned. "But you visited while I lived with Cailleach."

"Aye. She's not a Celt. For all I know they tried to keep me out, but she overruled them. Remember, she and I developed a working relationship. It might have made her more inclined to stand up for me."

I filed the problem away, determined to ask Arianrhod for details the following day. If I were cautious, picked my words with care, I might get an answer.

"You're here now." I straddled his lap so I faced him. "It's all that matters."

He threaded his arms around my back. "I've missed you. How are things going here?"

A tiny bit of my joy at seeing him faded. I had no idea how much progress I'd made, or how far I was from Arianrhod's goals. She'd never shared them with me. For all I knew, she'd still be parceling out magical assignments a century from now.

"That bad?" A corner of his mouth curled downward.

I shook my head. "Not bad. Different, is all. With Cailleach, I always knew where I stood."

"And here?" he prodded.

Wanting to be fair, I replied, "It's been a lot better since she found Hedrek for me, but I still have no idea how much

I've accomplished and how much lies ahead. Some days, it seems I could be here forever and still not absorb everything."

He angled his head to one side. "Not sure any of us ever come to the end of augmenting our skills." After a thoughtful pause, he added, "The question is at which point you no longer need a mentor-in-residence."

Hedrek squawked agreement—or something—from where he perched over the bowl of nuts.

"Let's not talk about any of that." I tightened my hold on him and tucked my head into the hollow between his shoulder and collarbone. He stroked my hair; my body truly relaxed for the first time since I'd arrived at Caer Sidi. We rocked against one another. Loving could wait until we were alone. For now, simply holding him, feeling the hard planes of his chest against my breasts and his thighs beneath my legs was enough.

"I've missed you," I murmured.

"Good to hear." He nuzzled my neck, breath warm against my skin.

Hedrek spread his wings and floated through the open window. For once he didn't hoot or make any kind of noise. Kind of him to sense our need to be alone.

Blake strung kisses up my neck until his lips landed on mine. Firm, demanding, and sensual as hell, his kiss reminded me of all the times we'd gotten lost in one another, shutting out the world.

My body responded in an instant, nipples hardening, thighs growing slick with heat and need. He'd barely touched me, and lust had already ignited between us. My fingers were still twined in his hair. I opened my mouth to his curious tongue and sparred with it as I'd done hundreds of times before.

Despite the familiarity, this was different. I felt whole for the first time in a long while, as if an elemental part of me had returned and clicked into place. I'd always prided myself on my independence. What in the hell had happened to make me so needy?

Blake broke our kiss. "No need to think it to death," he murmured in Gaelic.

And then I remembered one of his less savory habits. "You're in my mind." Even though I tried, I wasn't able to gin up any outrage. He was welcome in my mind, my body, and every other space I occupied.

"Of course, darling. No place I'd rather be, and—"

The door of my chamber slammed against the stops. Arianrhod stomped into the room, hands on her hips. "How in the fuck did you get in here?" she demanded.

Blake glanced up and arched a dark brow. "Nice to see you too," he said jauntily.

The goddess clomped closer. "I never said shit about it being nice to see you. What I asked"—she paused for emphasis—"is how you got into Caer Sidi?"

"I have my ways." He offered an enigmatic smile that told me he wasn't about to implicate Hedrek.

Arianrhod was close enough to poke his shoulder with an index finger. "Take those 'ways' and leave the way you came."

I've rarely seen Blake truly angry, but it rolled off him in waves as he shot to his feet and stood face to face with the goddess. "You have no right to speak to me in that fashion. Show me the respect due a Sidhe prince."

"Why?" She squared her shoulders. "You broke into my stronghold. Why you're little better than a common thief, and—"

"Stop right there," Blake thundered, "or Abria and I will take our leave."

"You can't do that," Arianrhod sputtered.

Time for me to jump into the fray. I stood too and said, "Watch us."

I was used to the goddess's intense stare. This time, it heated up a few notches as it bored into me. "Now is not a time to allow personal matters to intrude, child. You have a task, a critical one. You're nowhere near ready—"

"What task?" Blake cut in. "And while we're at it, whose idea was it to trap me in an arcane version of Warcraft? If I hadn't figured out you'd snared me, I'd still be there moving puerile pieces around an imaginary gameboard. The last thing I remember was swimming into Cailleach's underwater castle. Before I woke up and understood what was going on, that is."

Interesting. So that was what happened to him. "Cailleach wouldn't have tricked you. Not willingly," I said and linked hands with Blake. Together, we stared at Arianrhod. Either she'd pony up credible answers, or I was out of here. Ley lines or no ley lines. Training be damned; she wasn't the only teacher in all the worlds.

"So that's how it is," she muttered, clearly having helped herself to my thoughts.

No reason to deny anything, so I didn't. Neither did I

voice a caustic comment about it getting damned crowded inside my mind.

"Acolytes were more grateful in my time, more biddable too," she spat.

I resisted an urge to roll my eyes. "Yeah, things have changed. A lot," I agreed. "Will you answer Blake or no?"

Silence stretched through the room. As I thought about it, no wonder Hedrek had made good on his exit. With the supreme sensitivity of his kind, he'd no doubt sensed Arianrhod on the move. If I left, I hoped he'd choose to accompany us.

Words crowded the back of my throat. I held onto them. Arianrhod had come to a choice point. Nothing I said would make any difference. Either she'd accept me as more of an equal, or Blake and I would leave. It might take longer to ferret out if the task before me ran deeper than setting ley lines to rights, but I couldn't stand by while she denigrated Blake.

All the reasons I hated the Celts roared to the forefront. Still, I held silence.

Arianrhod turned away from us, hands on her hips as she stared out of a bank of windows.

Blake squeezed my fingers. *"I know the task,"* I sent in shielded mind speech. Arianrhod could intercept it, but she was caught between fury and practicality and probably wouldn't bother.

"Is it doable?" He pressed my hand once more.

I gave a small shrug because I truly had no idea.

We stood there for a long time, so long I shifted my weight from foot to foot. Finally, Arianrhod turned to face us. "This"—she paused for emphasis—"is why I did not want you here."

She didn't exactly point at Blake, but her meaning was crystal clear.

He narrowed his eyes, keeping his gaze fixed on the goddess. "I'm here now, and I'm not leaving unless I can come and go. I have naught against you training Abria, but I claim rights to spend time with her while she is in residence."

"Why, you arrogant—" she sputtered.

Blake waved a dismissive hand. I cringed, waiting for her to smite him—or whatever the Celts did when they were displeased. Scratch that. Furious was closer to the mark. Arianrhod's pale cheeks sported ruddy blotches. Interesting. She'd always been so disengaged, I'd wondered if anything got her going.

"Your choice," Blake went on, his words bland.

I was proud of him. After giving in to his temper, he had himself well under control and made no bones about refusing to fall into line as a second-class citizen.

"I must consult with the others," she muttered darkly before vanishing in a blaze of violet light.

My eyes widened. Could it be this simple to drive her from her home?

She won't be gone for long, I corrected myself. No way would she leave her domicile unguarded with two inferior beings roaming its halls.

Blake wrapped an arm around my shoulders and swung me to face him. "How long do you expect consulting with the other Celts will take?"

"No idea. She hasn't left since my arrival."

A corner of his mouth turned upward just before he lowered his lips over mine. I'd have laughed, but I was too caught up in the brush of his flesh against my own. So like Blake to never let an opportunity slip by.

I could read his thoughts without bothering to plumb them. His hands slipped the length of my spine to cup the globes of my ass. When he drew me against him, the swell of his erection pressed into my belly. His tongue explored the interior of my mouth.

I gave myself up to the sheer nearness of him. Sexual heat had been a driving factor from the moment he hailed me as I galloped across moorlands. Then, he'd worn his human glamour. He was plenty hot that way, but I far preferred his true form. Silky wings wrapped me in gossamer splendor. Sturdier than they looked, they provided a private cocoon shielding us from the rest of the world. Not that it was a problem here where we were the only two life forms for leagues, but those wings added a coziness factor.

We'd had public sex plenty of times, wings and a healthy jot of illusion concealing our activities from prying eyes. Graphic imagery fueled my arousal. I was lost in kissing him, drowning in sensation as he strung kisses along my neck. Meanwhile, he'd tugged my T-shirt out of the way, exposing my breasts. No bras here. The only ones who looked at me were Arianrhod and Hedrek. Neither of them cared if my tits were unbound.

I snaked a hand between us and gripped the hot, hard length of him. His eager member twitched against my hand.

Panting and moaning, we ground our bodies together, desperate for more of one another.

So many clothes in between. Magic could shred them, but repair was a different story. He bit my lower lip. I bit back, tasting blood. Maybe the Celts mixed Vampire into my making because it stoked my lust. Blake jerked my shirt over my head and tossed it aside. Bending his head, he scribed lazy circles around a nipple with his tongue.

Long-denied sensuality roared through me along with a look-ma-no-hands climax that made the room spin. I didn't remember unzipping his trousers, but his dick was in my hand, skin to skin. Drops coated the velvety head. Sinking to my knees, I took him in my mouth.

Nothing gentle about my ministrations. I stroked his shaft hard and sure, knowing exactly how he liked it. He groaned and muttered in Gaelic as he thrust into my mouth. We'd been so deprived, he came almost as quickly as I had. Thick gouts of salty semen painted the interior of my mouth.

I swallowed greedily and wished for more. After licking him clean, I scooted up his body. We ended up on the floor with me on top, hips grinding against his still-hard erection.

"Hussy." He grinned up at me.

"You like your women loose. Admit it." I swiped my tongue across his lower lip.

"Looser the better, wench." He grappled with the fastenings on my pants.

"Don't you two ever give it a rest?" Arianrhod's stentorian tones had the same effect a bucket of ice water might have.

I craned my neck, trying to see her, but Blake's wings were in the way. "How long have you been here?" I tried for dignity and failed.

"You should have made your presence known," Blake cut in. Beneath the ashes of his lust, he sounded pissed.

"This is what I get for attempting to extend consideration while you rut on the floors of my very house?"

Fuck me. I tucked Blake's dick back into his trousers, got to my feet, and faced Arianrhod. "You're jealous," I tossed in her face.

"Why, you impertinent wretch." She shook a finger in my face.

About that time, I realized I was missing my shirt and scooped it off the floor, donning it hastily.

Blake stood next to me. "What was the consensus?" he asked smoothly.

Oh right. Consensus. It was why she'd left. My brain was so addled by his nearness, I'd forgotten everything except the joy we wrung from one another's bodies.

"There wasn't one." Exasperation rode beneath her tone.

Before either of us could question her further, she crooked a finger. "Come. We must talk." Turning, she hurried from the room.

After exchanging a look with Blake, I murmured, "We don't have to obey her."

He shook his head. "Nay, lass. In this instance, 'tis better if we do." He extended a hand. After a thoughtful pause, I took it, and we followed a generous trail of Celtic magic. Arianrhod wasn't taking any chances we'd get lost. Consideration wasn't an element in her wheelhouse, so Blake might be onto something with his insistence we humor her demand for an audience.

Breath chittered through my teeth as I hustled along. Left to my own devices, I'd have beat a track for Underhill, but even I recognized balls were in motion. Ones that would determine if I had a future, and what it would look like.

I curled one hand into a fist. That future had better include Blake. His scent clung to me, teasing my nerve endings with promises of more than the appetizer we'd stolen earlier.

What if it doesn't? a sly inner voice inquired.

It has to. My silent reply was firm, determined. I'm nobody's patsy. I'd play along, fulfill my role as best I could, but Blake was a dealbreaker. He had to be part of—everything. Or I was out of here.

CHAPTER 8
BLAKE

Leaving was tempting. The Celts always made my skin crawl, like I'd brushed up against something slimy. Still, I had an investment—albeit a slight one—in maintaining decent relations with them. As envoy for my people, it would be the height of irresponsibility to annoy Arianrhod. She and her kinsmen could make life miserable for the Sidhe by disrupting our connection to the natural world. Workarounds weren't impossible, but I could spare a few moments to not have to end up deep in damage control.

That's the thing about indulging in anger. It's ever so satisfying in the moment, but you pay for that indulgence many times over. I'd been stuffing my resentment toward the Celts for so many eons, one more go-round was meaningless.

Speaking of damage control, I admit I'd held my breath

when Abria tossed the part about being jealous in Arianrhod's face. Abria has a temper to go with her flame-red
hair, and she was fully capable of hurling a catty comment
about the goddess's sham virgin status in her face.

I'd been ready to step in, talk over her if need be, but it
hadn't been necessary.

Power drew us along. Arianrhod wasn't taking any
chances we'd change our minds. The moment we started
after her, we couldn't have left if wanted.

Well, we could have, but the price would have been
steep, and it would have blown the fragile détente I'd
worked so hard to establish to smithereens.

Abria squeezed my hand. I squeezed back. Almost as tall
as me with a lithe, athletic build, she was one striking
woman. Hair flowed well past her waist, and her almond-
shaped green eyes lent her the appearance of a large feline
on the prowl. Rounded breasts and a high tight ass would
have given any man an instant hard-on. Said breasts were
bouncing beneath her shirt as we trotted along.

My errant appendage had scarcely settled after our too
brief skirmish. Visions of Abria sans clothing sent blood
flooding my nether regions. Not good. I needed to think, not
lust after my almost-mate.

It appeared we had a spot of semi-private time. Caer Sidi
was huge. Or maybe Arianrhod was leading us in circles in
the same way you tired a horse and made it more biddable
at the end of a lunge line.

"What exactly do you know about this task of yours?" I
asked.

Abria flashed a sideways glance my way and nodded. "Not all that much. I just found out about it since I arrived here."

I waited, but she turned her gaze straight ahead, russet brows knitted together. "Are you going to tell me?" I pressed.

She screwed her mouth into a frown. "Of course. Sorry. I guess I assumed you knew since you've lived practically forever."

I gave a small shrug. "Maybe I do know, but if it's true, I haven't made the connection with you."

"That's because your mind's always in the gutter."

"And yours isn't?"

She laughed softly. It lightened the mood, and I joined her.

"The short version is my birth, er making, created some cosmic disturbance in the ley lines and made it harder for mages to wield power. They blamed me and have been hunting me ever since."

Her recitation struck a vaguely familiar note. I'd stumbled across the story, but hadn't realized she sat at its center. "Mages, yes," I murmured, "but it never affected the Sidhe."

"Wonder why not?" Abria ground to a halt and glanced from side to side. "We passed this spot before. Where in the hell is she leading us?"

Indeed. Was she even still out there somewhere? Or had she simply laid a track and moved on? Stopping posed its own set of problems. My feet wanted to keep on keeping on.

"Don't you feel that?" I asked.

"Feel what?" Abria had switched from looking about to turning in a full circle.

How to describe it? "Arianrhod's magic tugs at me."

"Interesting. I seem to be immune to it." Cupping both hands around her mouth, she shouted, "Arianrhod. What manner of game is this?"

I winced, but I was proud of her. I'd have been far more diplomatic, less bold. Hell, if Abria hadn't stopped, I'd still be chasing Celtic magic—and getting nowhere. Deference to the gods is hardwired into my makeup, and something I need to jettison. Times have changed drastically. They're no longer worthy of such respect.

Perhaps they never were.

The goddess sashayed out of a nearby doorway. She'd taken the time to change into an iridescent silvery robe that sparkled in the strange, muted light of Caer Sidi. A brilliant red sash spanned her midsection; power spilled from a jeweled scepter clutched in her right hand.

Setting it down, she rubbed her hands together. Rings set with gemstones graced most of her fingers. "Good. Good. We've all had time to think about this," she began.

"Speak for yourself." Diplomacy be damned. I was done being polite. "We could have crafted our own thinking time without being dragged around your realm."

"But this was so much more productive," she purred. "I was curious how long it would take you two to figure things out."

"Figure what out?" Abria's eyes sparked with ire.

"That you were free to exit your impromptu tour of Caer Sidi. What else?"

I unclenched my jaw. None of this power-play crap was important. "Never mind that." I tried for a firm tone, one that would have sent my minions scuttling for cover. "What was the outcome of your discussion with your kinsmen?"

"I want to know too," Abria spoke up.

The scepter shone more brightly; the goddess picked it up, cradling it in the crook of one arm. To be on the safe side, I draped a hasty ward over Abria and me.

Arianrhod arched a fair brow. "What's the matter, Sidhe? Don't you trust me?"

"You've given me little reason to." Yeah. My diplomacy just crashed and burned.

Laughter rolled from her. When it quieted, she said, "There might be hope for you yet, Sidhe."

I bit back a curt response about goddesses who live in glass houses not throwing stones.

"Enough sparring." She dropped her arms to her sides. The scepter took on a bluish glow. "No one agreed. With anything. It means we are on our own determining next steps. 'Tisn't surprising since no one wanted aught to do with Abria's lessons other than Ceridwen. Naturally, I couldn't locate her. And the Morrigan is stuck in Hell. Not my first choice to visit."

"She'll get out of there someday," Abria said. "When she does, she'll be livid."

Arianrhod chuckled. "Och, child. She already is. For the sake of humankind, she'd best not break her bonds. If she does, the battle crow will wreak havoc, turning son against father and brothers against one another."

"Not important," I gritted. "What happens next with Abria?"

Arianrhod aimed a pointed glance down her aquiline nose at me. "Before you showed up, we were managing fine."

"Your opinion," Abria cut in. "I want him here at least some of the time. He amplifies my power."

I draped an arm around her shoulder. "I must be free to come and go as my other duties allow."

Hedrek chose that moment to swoop in from somewhere. After scribing a few lazy circles around our heads, he landed on a nearby table that materialized out of nowhere. Hooting softly, he clacked his beak together.

Aye, if the fucking owl had the run of the place, no reason I couldn't show up every week or so. To strengthen my earlier statement, I added, "If it's inconvenient having me drop in, Abria and I will return to Underhill. You'd be most welcome to train her there."

"With the Sidhe?"

Her intimation we were peasants rankled. "Aye. Last I checked the Sidhe inhabit Underhill. Along with Fae and the odd witch from time to time."

Another hoot was followed by, "I'm flexible."

I'd figured he could talk. Most magical animals hold that ability, but his voice was a surprise. Deep and melodic, it soothed the ragged edges of my temper.

Arianrhod pointed the scepter his way. "You'll do as I say."

A flurry of hoots was probably the equivalent of avian laughter. "Since when?" Hedrek inquired.

If he'd been closer, I'd have stroked his feathers. "Good for you," I mouthed and watched the scepter develop a reddish hue. If I were her, I wouldn't want an accoutrement that displayed my moods.

"How much more instruction will I actually require?" Abria let go of my hand and squared her shoulders.

"Depends how well you apply yourself," Arianrhod replied stiffly.

"Pretend I'm perfect. How long, then?"

"Hard to say, child." The scepter clattered to the floor, and the goddess moved closer to Abria. "If you attempt to alter the lines before you're fully ready, they'll eat you up alive."

Fascinating. Beneath the goddess's annoyingly brash presumptuousness, she cared about Abria. A lot. The top layer of my irritation sloughed off. "You'd be welcome in Underhill. Many of my people revere you."

Her unnerving gaze, one eye silver, the other gold, bored into me. I held myself open beneath her scrutiny, so she'd see my words as truth rather than empty rhetoric.

A corner of her mouth twitched. "I don't suppose you'll be persuaded to remain gone."

"Good guess." I spread my hands in front of me. "Let's start fresh, shall we? I'm willing to forget the trick you played on me—"

"But it was kind. You enjoyed yourself." A pause before she added, "We could have done so much worse."

"I'm sure you could have. It's never kind to delude someone, or trap them against their will." Before she ginned up a reply, I went on. "I meant what I said about a reset. About starting over. There's been little love lost between our people. We—you and I —can't alter that, but we can refresh what flows between us.

"Both of us lo—" I recalibrated. "Both of us care for Abria, want the best for her. How can we accomplish that if we're at one another's throats?" I'd said enough. Sometimes extra words only get in the way.

"You might have a point, Sidhe." Arianrhod's voice was rough, and she made shooing motions. "Back to Underhill. I'll find you when I'm ready."

"But I'll need to know when that is," Abria protested. "So I can be certain to be there."

"Do you honestly believe I can't locate you no matter where you are?"

Color stained Abria's fair cheeks, and then she surprised me by pelting toward the goddess and wrapping her arms around her. "Thank you. For everything. For dreaming me in the first place. For caring enough to take the time you have."

The goddess stood stock still, a shocked expression twisting her features. Slowly, it melted into a smile, and she hugged Abria back.

I haven't been leading the Sidhe all these years for nothing. We'd reached a perfect exit point. I summoned a travel spell, had it ready when Abria let go of the goddess and walked to my side. Hedrek left his table to perch on her shoulder.

Telling Arianrhod I'd look forward to her visit would have been disingenuous, so I didn't. We'd come far closer to establishing the start of a workable partnership than I'd dared hope, but for it to flourish would require care on both sides.

"Wait," Arianrhod called. Moments later, she thrust a battered valise into Abria's arms.

"My things. Thank you."

"You're welcome back here any time, child." The goddess pointed a long-nailed index finger at Hedrek and me. "The two of you will need to ask permission, just like any other visitor to my realm."

"Of course, my lady." It was easier to be pleasant to her now she'd dropped her guard and shown a tiny corner of her true nature. Invoking a power word, I kindled my spell, and we traded the halls of Caer Sidi for the darkness of the in-between place.

Hedrek hooted softly. Abria snuggled close. We were so far from home free it wasn't even a distant glimmer, but this was a start. "How do you feel about planning a wedding?" I asked.

"Wait. Aren't you supposed to get down on one knee? Offer me a ring worth millions?"

"I could do both those things, but if you're not interested—"

She elbowed me briskly. "Who said I wasn't interested? We'll get cracking as soon as we get home."

Home. I loved the sound of the word on her tongue because it included me and mine.

"Best bird?" Hedrek squawked.

"Why not?" Abria laughed. "You can join up with the

unicorns. It's antiquated, but Becca and her herd will want to give me away..."

They chattered of this and that as I guided us until I felt the tug of Underhill. This time I wasn't picky. Anywhere in my realm would do.

"There you are," Kirwan and Breanne said almost in unison as the dust from my spell settled.

"You're needed." Kirwan sounded rattled.

"Council has been convened and awaits your presence." Breanne hesitated before adding, "Some are already convinced you won't show." Her stilted formal tones weren't like her; worry sluiced through me. After my tense exchange with Arianrhod, I'd hoped for a respite.

Aye, hope and a shilling wouldn't even buy me a cup of tea.

Hedrek floated from Abria's shoulders to Breanne's. She cooed at the owl.

Kirwan set a quick pace. We followed him. So much for weddings. "If you're tired," I told Abria, "you can wait in my rooms."

"We're in this together," she said firmly. "If it weren't for me, you'd have been here. The least I can do is offer my apologies to your people."

Love for her raced through me. Not the most useful of emotions, and not one that fit whatever misfortune had intruded this time.

The open doors of the council chamber loomed ahead. The din of restive voices, coupled with energy so tense it marred Underhill's usually placid ambience, made me suspect Kirwan and Breanne had underplayed what faced us. Regardless, it didn't require seer magic to recognize once I stepped through those doors my well-balanced world was about to come tumbling down.

Fierce strength spilled through me. Whatever this was, I'd protect my people. No matter what the cost.

CHAPTER 9
ABRIA

I'd met Kirwan and Breanne before. Though they didn't come out and say it, I was certain they blamed me for Blake's extended absences. Rightly so. Were it not for me, he'd have been here taking care of business. Never mind he'd let things slide for a few centuries, but a Cait Sidhe rebellion convinced him he couldn't rule in absentia.

Breanne was tall and blocky. Were it not for breasts, she'd have been built like a burly man. When last I'd seen her, her head had been shaved. Now, a halo of spiky white curls stuck out at odd angles setting off the rough planes of her face. Gray eyes didn't miss much. Leather pants and a matching buff-colored tunic swathed her impressive bulk. As usual, her feet were bare, and a wicked-looking axe was strapped across her back.

In contrast, Kirwan looked a bit like a Shar-pei. Wrinkles

upon wrinkles covered his aged face. Mostly bald, a fringe of gray hair sat just above his ears lending him a monkish appearance. In line with that, he wore a dark-brown robe and rope sandals.

As we drew closer to the council chamber, waves of unrest buffeted me. Hedrek must have felt them too because he was back on my shoulders, wings opening and closing slowly.

Perhaps I should take Blake up on his suggestion and sit this one out in his rooms. All my presence would do is serve as a reminder Blake was not only mating outside the blood, but also that he'd sloughed off on his duties because of it.

Chicken, an inner critic noted.

Damn straight. Maybe not cowardly as much as not wanting to make things worse by flaunting my presence in a roomful of Sidhe who'd never been overly fond of me. Not that they had a corner on that market. I'm an oddball, one-of-a-kind mage. Because I was different, nobody trusted me. Centuries ago, it bothered me, but I've moved past caring what anyone thinks.

Besides, I had animals to fill the void. They beat mages hands down any day of any week.

About fifty feet separated me from the door. If I was going to cut and run, I had to go now. Blake had already offered me an out. Maybe there'd been more to it than him being kind. Maybe he didn't want me here, and—

Stop. Just stop.

I don't usually take my own advice. In this instance, though, I did.

If I was on the verge of marrying Blake, I refused to start our life together by running from his people. Determined. I straightened my spine and passed beneath the lintel. It might have been my imagination, but the tenor of many conversations developed even more ominous undertones.

Blake clapped his hands smartly together and loped across the big room to an empty spot in the center of a richly carved table placed laterally. The chamber was elegant with open beams and marble-topped tables. Over a hundred Sidhe were ranged through the room in groups of twos, threes, and fives. Most stood, ignoring chairs they could have sat on.

"About time...Regent," a man's dry voice called. Stunning like all Sidhe, his golden hair was plaited against his head in many small rows. Violet eyes sat above chiseled cheekbones and a sculpted chin. A cream-colored silk robe sashed in deep blue swathed his lithe frame. Gemstones had been woven into his braids. Rings graced several fingers, and a large, clear onyx pendant hung from a chain around his neck.

"I'm here now, Lewin." Blake faced the assemblage. His black hair was mussed, his garments travel-stained. I knew him well enough to see signs of strain around his dark eyes. Should I join him? Offer visible support?

Probably not the best idea until I had more of a sense which way the Sidhe winds were blowing.

"Rather than chastising me," Blake addressed Lewin, "your voice would find far better use telling me what's happened."

Yeah, we'd all like to know.

I kept that thought to myself. From wedding planning to a war council was a quantum leap. My scrappy side rose to the challenge. One advantage to always being alone was I've never counted on anyone to bail me out of anything. Until Blake came along, I was a regular one-woman-band—unless you counted unicorns and other magical beasts who occasionally showed up at opportune moments.

Lewin swung and pointed at me. "Convenient. You brought the problem along. All we have to do is hand her over, and—"

"Silence!" Blake thundered. "'Tis my intended you refer to. Show some respect."

"You show some," Lewin countered. "After millennia of bachelorhood, the least you could do is marry within our ranks."

My jaw tightened, teeth clenched together to keep me from marching up to the Sidhe who'd requested my head on a platter and challenging him to a duel. While I kept control of myself, I had no such luck with the owl. Hedrek launched himself from my shoulders and flew straight at Lewin, who threw an arm up to block the assault.

"That's right," he sneered. "You command animals. Call this one off. It's an outrage to be attacked in my own halls."

"I didn't send him. He thinks for himself," I shot back.

Meanwhile Hedrek circled behind Lewin and pecked the side of his neck. Blood flowed, staining the robe's collar. Hooting something that sounded like a victory cry, he circled, clearly intent on more.

"Hedrek!" Blake vaulted across the table and wove between groups of Sidhe. "Leave off."

"But he insulted Abria," the owl said, fanning his wings to slow his forward speed.

"I don't like that part, either." Blake reached the owl's vicinity and held out an arm. Hedrek landed, beak clacking. "Would someone tell me why Abria has turned into a sacrificial goat?"

I snickered at his choice of words. I'd much rather be a sacrificial goddess, but it was splitting hairs.

Breanne still stood near the entrance. "The Cait paid us a visit," she said in a deep, gravelly voice.

"Aye, along with a pet demon or two," Kirwan added, his voice reminiscent of a pile of long-dry leaves rustling in the wind.

"They reminded us of something we'd forgotten," Breanne went on. "Abria is the reason all mages but the Sidhe have to work harder to wield power. Her arrival coincided with an alteration in magic's underpinnings."

"Happened so long ago, none of us made the connection." Kirwan picked up the tale. "At the time, we didn't recognize what was happening. Since the Celts took pains to hide Abria away, most of us didn't believe she existed."

"We'd heard rumors of an animal mage," Breanne said when Kirwan stopped to take a breath. "But by the time any of us ran across her so much time had passed we'd forgotten the myths surrounding her birth."

"See?" Lewin dusted his hands together but kept distance between himself and Hedrek.

"See what?" Blake's question could have etched runnels in granite.

"'Tis simple enough," Lewin plowed on, although he didn't sound as certain as he had. "The Cait are making the rounds. Soon, everyone will know where to find Abria. Simpler to hand her over. She's not one of us."

A rising tide of voices filled the chamber. Some cheered, others booed. I wished I could sink through the stone floor.

"No one is handing Abria to anyone." Blake's voice rang through the room. "No one. Am I clear?"

I rolled my shoulders back and projected my voice. "I could leave," I suggested. "Out of sight, out of mind."

"That wasn't the deal," Lewin mumbled.

Blake catapulted to where Lewin stood, Hedrek still on his arm. "What deal? You're not authorized to bind the Sidhe to anything."

"But I'm keeping us safe, out of another war," Lewin protested. "You're never here. Someone has to make decisions."

"I can just see the altruism dripping off your halo," Blake sneered. "Decisions are why we have a council. Last I checked, you weren't part of it."

Hedrek leapt into the air and flew in lazy circles, reminding everyone he was my personal bodyguard. At least for today. If the Sidhe who'd toss me out like yesterday's trash didn't like it, I could call in reinforcements. Wolves. Unicorns. Maybe a dragon or two, although I hadn't actually seen one for the last five hundred years. Hell, Cailleach had my back. So did Arianrhod. We hadn't burned that bridge. It would serve Lewin and his buddies right to face her wrath when she showed up and discovered I'd turned into collateral damage.

Breanne strode to Blake's side. "If we do not comply, the Cait have promised war. Except this time, they'll bring allies to the field."

"Since when do we fold in the face of threats?" His voice reverberated through the hall. "We have never"—he paused for emphasis—"never allowed ourselves to be manipulated by threats. And we will not begin now."

A flurry of hoots reminded me Hedrek still circled the chamber.

"It's not like she's one of us." Lewin's patrician face took on a mulish aspect.

"I wouldn't turn a cockroach over to the Cait," Blake retorted. He spread his arms and stomped in a circle, eyeing the assemblage. "Our council has never voted to turn an innocent over to our enemies. If any of you are so inclined, the door is that way. Take an hour to gather your belongings and leave Underhill. If you do, she will be barred to you forever, so think long and hard before you decide."

I stood tall, but it wasn't easy under the glare of hostile sets of eyes. I got it. They viewed me as the problem, as the hussy who'd seduced their leader away from the straight and narrow. No matter how competently I slung magic about—and I was pretty damned skilled—I'd never be a Sidhe. My jaws had clenched once more. The injustice of being ostracized for something that wasn't my fault stung, but I'd be damned if I'd let them know they'd hurt me.

Lewin strode across the hall and out the door. Two others followed in his wake. I waited, but no one else walked away. Breath caught in my throat. Three was a manageable number. If half the assemblage had surged from the room, I'd have done my best to convince Blake to recant. Simpler for me to leave than a lion's share of his kin.

"By the goddess's grace, most of you have retained your senses," Blake said. "The easy way isn't usually best. If we capitulated to the Cait's demands, they'd view us as weak. Abria would only be the first in a series of escalating ultimatums. They'll assume if we gave in once, we'd do so again and again until the Cait ruled Underhill like they've always yearned to do.

"Abria will be my mate," he went on. "If anyone objects, let's get it out on the table now."

Still in full defiance mode, I slid my gaze over the room. Some shied away from my appraisal; others stared back with varying degrees of acceptance.

"If you're set on that path," Breanne spoke up, "best solemnize it now so Underhill will recognize Abria as one of ours and protect her."

Words pressed against my throat. I almost told her I didn't need anyone or anything beyond my animal honor guard to safeguard me. Wisdom ruled the day, and I kept quiet. I was the new kid on the block. Worse, I was the reason war was descending on the Sidhe.

Maybe.

My take on the Cait was they were a bunch of bully blowhards who crumpled like a pack of crooked cards under pressure, but I wasn't about to voice that thought, either.

"Agreed," Blake was saying. "Tomorrow at dawn works."

My eyes widened. Dawn was for births, deaths, and

duels. I was still standing, thunderstruck, when Sidhe flowed around me as they plopped into chairs facing the dais. Blake and eleven others took their places at the long table facing the room.

I sank into a chair so I wouldn't stand out like a sore thumb. I'd already caused way more than my fair share of problems in Sidhe-land. Hedrek lighted next to me and leaned against my side. I stroked his feathers and murmured, *"Thanks."*

"You are mine to defend. Arianrhod tasked me thus."

I did a double take. Not only had the goddess found the bird for me, she'd apparently sworn him to look out for my wellbeing. *"I release you from that promise,"* I told him.

He pecked at my hand, but gently. Good thing, his curved beak could have meted out significant damage.

Blake was gathering additional information about the threat we faced. Use of the inclusive pronoun made me smile softly. I hadn't ever been part of a *we* that wasn't exclusively made up of fur, feathers, or scales before—if I didn't count my recent instruction from Cailleach and Arianrhod.

Thinking about animals brought me up short. They'd want to be part of my wedding. All of them, not that it was practical. I bent my head close to the owl and asked if he could let as many know as was feasible. After bobbing his head, he flew from the room.

And not just animals. Birgit, a witch who'd been through a lot with me, and Cailleach would surely want to be here too. From there, my thoughts stretched in many directions. What would I wear? Did it even matter? It wasn't as if I were one of those silly human females who'd dreamt of frothy white gowns trimmed in acres of Venetian lace.

Conversation swirled around me. Blake and his council were laying out the bones of their next steps against the Cait. I should be paying close attention, but my mind was a muddle. I couldn't recall the last time I'd slept, and my eyes were hot and gritty.

The brush of feathers against my cheek jolted me awake. Crap. I must have shut my eyes for a moment—maybe two or three. Tough to tell since the Sidhe were still at it. Blake was drawing on something like a sheet of crystal suspended in the air. Magical version of an Etch A Sketch.

The comparison made me smile.

Hedrek sat on the floor next to my chair. He was so large his head was about the same level as my midsection. I wanted to ruffle his silky, golden feathers, but he might not have appreciated the familiarity. After all, we didn't know one another all that well.

Before me, the drawing Blake had been working on came to life. Clearly a battle diagram, rows of combatants moved in complex patterns before vanishing off the edge only to reappear elsewhere. The Sidhe had left their seats and were ranged in front of the moving display pointing at this, that, or the other thing and shouting suggestions in their language. My linguistic capabilities had improved, but I still missed some of what had to be salient points.

Ashamed I'd drifted off—and hoping no one had noticed —I stood and made my way to the front of the room. If I was going to be Blake's mate, my place was by his side, not moldering in a seat halfway across the room. I stopped at the rear of the last row of Sidhe and focused on the mock battle playing out on the screen.

I've mostly worked alone, but I'm no stranger to strategy. Pressing my tongue against the back of my teeth, I examined the display depicting a very traditional brute-force approach. Might have worked if the enemy were other than Cait Sidhe. They were cats first, faeries second. They still thought like cats; fought like them too. We'd be far better served with sneaky and underhanded.

I bit my lower lip. Did I dare raise my hand? Or jump into one of many conversational gaps with ideas? I didn't want to contradict Blake—or his deputies or whatever the other council members called themselves.

The discussion was winding down, given nods and murmurs. If I was going to stick my oar in the water, it was now or never. Prudence dictated keeping a low profile—at least until tomorrow's ceremony solidified my bond with Blake. But I've never been like that. The Cait may be devious, but I play with my cards on the table.

The Sidhe were on the edge of accepting me into their ranks. I did not want it to be under false pretenses. Neither did I want them to accuse me of concealing my stripes until it was too late to undo the mating ceremony. Magical beings don't wed all that often, but when they—er, we—do, it's permanent.

Far better to be who I was than for Blake to share blood with me before he discovered sometimes my opinions would diverge from his. Eh, he probably already knew as much, but his subjects didn't. Before I thought things to death, I threaded my way through the throng until I stood in front of him.

Requesting permission to speak was ridiculous, so I simply said, "I have an idea."

Dark eyes latched onto mine. "We're nearly done here," Blake informed me.

I nodded. "Yeah. Figured that one out. I'm offering a couple of thoughts is all."

This time, many sets of eyes switched focus, falling on me. I pushed my shoulders back. Perhaps I should have stayed in my chair, but that train had left the station. Hedrek was back in the air- circling the crowd and hooting softly.

Breanne made come along motions with long, tapering fingers. "Out with it."

Not much of an invitation, but things weren't going to improve. Plotting war against distant relatives couldn't be easy. I nodded silent thanks her way and turned to face rows of Sidhe.

"I wouldn't presume to know your kinsmen better than you." I tried to strike a conciliatory note.

"Then why say anything at all?" a man shouted from the rear of the crowd.

Good question. Because I'm a control freak? Because I have a tough time standing back and letting someone make a mistake.

I don't know that their approach is ill-conceived. Not for sure, an inner voice popped up.

"Abria?" Blake prodded. I knew him well enough to hear how exhausted he was. Leading the Sidhe held all the allure of herding hyenas.

Not many choices here. Either I backed down—and if I made that choice, why rock the applecart to start with? Or I tossed my two cents' worth on the table. Spreading my hands in front of me, I said, "Your enemy is known for their deviousness, yet you've designed a battle plan better suited to fighters such as yourselves..."

CHAPTER 10
BLAKE

I cringed when Abria started talking, but I was proud of her too. In truth, the cringing was aimed at my people more than her. We're an insular, stiff-necked lot and don't take kindly to suggestions from outsiders, no matter how well-intentioned.

Tomorrow morning's ceremony wouldn't make Abria any less of an outsider, but it was a start. Maybe in a couple of hundred years, some of the more openminded Sidhe would accept her and value her opinions.

Until then, she may as well have saved her breath and her time. She'd taken over the enchanted version of a whiteboard and was covering it with hieroglyphs. Given her limited battle experience, her grasp of the situation was surprisingly accurate.

Better than mine had been because she wasn't viewing the Cait through rose-colored glasses. Nay, to her they were conniving sons of bitches. I'd always nurtured the hope they'd see the light and return to the fold. Not overly likely, but leaders aren't supposed to give up on any of their subjects, fallen or otherwise.

Perhaps I was mistaken about my people discounting her message. No one was shouting her down or suggesting she was wasting their time.

"Depending on what you want," Abria continued as she sketched on the display, "striking fast and hard will maintain the element of surprise and enhance the odds of a quick defeat. The Cait are devious. It's where they eat, live, and breathe. To win, you'll need to anticipate which bit of fuckery they favor this round and beat them at their own game." She paused for emphasis. "If that's not your objective, if you'd prefer to toy with them, then my ideas won't work at all. But then, you'll be stuck fighting them forever."

"What do you have in mind?" Breanne asked in brusque tones. "Make it snappy and be specific. We've already been at this for a while."

Abria's fair cheeks developed red splotches that almost matched her hair. She had a temperamental side, and I tossed a silent prayer into the void that she'd keep a tight grip on her attitude.

Muscles danced beneath her jawline as she tilted her chin and faced Breanne. "The gist of my idea is that you're fluid and meet every thrust and parry the Cait present. Last time, you quit fighting the moment they retreated. See where that's gotten you? Since I have no idea how or when they'll strike next, I can't be more specific than that."

"We need spies," Kirwan spoke up.

I opened my mouth to protest we were certainly not

going to spy on our own but shut it just as quickly. The Cait may have been part of us, but not for a very long while. They're who'd thrown down the gauntlet. Hell, they'd tried to shut a primary portal into Underhill and taken down two changelings I'd set to guard it.

"How do you propose to manage spying?" Breanne arched a white brow Kirwan's way. "None of us can pass as Cait."

"I could round up a few cats," Abria murmured. "Probably even magical ones if I look hard enough. They're not Cait Sidhe, but surely the cat connection would be enough. Seems to me, the Cait will be hunting for additional warriors to shore up their ranks."

Breanne cocked her head to one side on her thick neck. "Cannon fodder. Brilliant, lass, simply brilliant."

I frowned as I mulled it over. "Don't they have servants already?" I asked the group.

Kirwan nodded. "Aye, but many are old, feeble, not good for much beyond menial tasks."

"How soon can you marshal your spies?" Breanne asked Abria.

"I'm not certain. A few days, perhaps a week. Where will you want them?"

Many sets of eyes settled on me, for all the good I'd be. After turning my hands palms upward, I said, "I have no idea where the Cait are keeping themselves these days."

"We know where they aren't," Breanne muttered.

Indeed, but applying a process of elimination could take a long while. I inhaled noisily. "I can try the link. If I'm careful—and they're not paying attention—I might get away with it."

"What link?" Abria asked.

"As regent, he holds links to all Sidhe," Kirwan explained.

"But if they know I'm looking for them," I cut in, "they'll just move and be far more careful to shield their whereabouts."

"How do you know they're not doing that now?" Abria asked.

I shrugged. "I won't until I hunt around. I'll see what I can accomplish as soon as we adjourn."

"And I'll identify a couple of volunteers, or try to," Abria said. She didn't sound as certain as she had earlier. Was she having second thoughts?

"Let me make sure I have this straight." Breanne's deep, growl of a voice grated across my ears. "We infiltrate their camp. As soon as our spy provides information, we launch an offensive."

Nods ran through the room. Good enough for now. We'd fill in the blank spots when we had more intel. Sidhe turned and filed from the chamber. I dismantled the magic keeping the display in place. Hedrek floated to Abria's shoulders.

She waited until only the three of us remained before saying. "I shouldn't have offered what I did. It's dangerous. What if the Cait figure things out and kill whomever I tapped for this mission?"

"Dangerous, but a brilliant idea," I agreed. "You'll be up front with any potential volunteers."

Abria shook her head. Flame-red hair danced around her

face. She looked tired with dark circles under her eyes and dirt smudges on her cheeks, but she had every right. Neither of us had slept in goddess only knew how long.

"Being honest isn't the point," she explained. "Animals will do anything for me, anything I request of them. It's how the bond works. In fact, they'll clamor to be the first to sign up no matter how dangerous it is because they love me."

She shut her eyes for a moment. When she opened them, she continued, "After I was trapped in that alley in Inverness and a wolf died defending me, I made a vow to never put any of my people in danger again."

My heart squeezed painfully in my chest. I understood completely. Walking close, I draped an arm around her shoulders, being careful not to disturb the owl who was hooting softly.

"I feel the same way about the Sidhe," I said. "Even the Cait, which is why we're at our current juncture. I've never given up hoping they'd see the light."

"They never will." Abria made a sour face.

"It's becoming clearer," I muttered. "Look, this is up to you. We could use the help, but if you've reconsidered, we'll come up with another way."

"Not reconsidered so much as rethinking things. Maybe I could go with them. It's not as if this will be a time-consuming project," she said.

I dropped my arm and spun until I faced her. The words that wanted out were, "Oh hell, no," but I caught myself and said, "Not the best idea."

"And why not?" She folded her arms under her breasts.

Aye, good thing I'd sat on my *oh hell, no* statement.

Try as I might, I couldn't come up with a decent response beyond me being selfish and wanting to keep her safe. Sort of the same way she felt about any cats she might recruit.

After a few moments passed where she may or may not have culled my thoughts, she nodded knowingly. "Either I go with them, or we develop another method to determine what the Cait have in mind."

An idea rolled around in my mind. "Roya might be willing to help."

Abria angled her head to one side, clearly searching for the name. Her green eyes widened. "The changeling who helped save my life. Isn't she in the *Dreaming*?"

I nodded. "The Cait caused her untold grief. She's been in the *Dreaming* long enough to heal, though."

Fingers waggled at me. Abria knew I hadn't shared everything in my head. "If Roya is willing," I said slowly, testing my idea as I went, "she could tell the Cait she's had time to think things over, that she'd much rather throw in her lot with them than us. She could paint me as a bastard who stuck her with guard duty for millennia with no recompense."

A corner of Abria's mouth twitched upward. "And then dumped her in the *Dreaming*. Out of sight, out of mind."

"Something like that." I raked fingers through my hair. "Nothing says we can't do both."

"Send Roya and a couple of cats?"

I nodded.

"There's still the problem of who's going to protect them if things head south." Abria blew out a breath. "You can't go.

Neither can I unless I'm cloaked the entire time." She made a face. "My magic is stronger, but not that much. Wards blow through power like nobody's business."

I held up a hand. "Give me a moment. Let's see if I can determine where they are. It could make a difference."

I retraced my steps to the dais and a hefty crystal orb. It would both strengthen my ability and shield my location. I hoped. It had been a long while since I used it to find any of my subjects. No need since they all lived in proximity to Underhill or the *Dreaming*.

Behind me, the scrape of a chair suggested Abria had settled into one. Good. She needed rest. I emptied my mind of everything except the task ahead. I'd have to be quick— and delicate. Not easy since I had no idea how far away the Cait had set up headquarters. If they were closer than I expected, I might use too much power and tip my hand.

On the other side of things, if I didn't employ sufficient magic and ended up floundering around, I'd reveal my intentions inadvertently. This might all be for naught, anyway. The Cait were well aware of my linkage to every Sidhe. For all I knew, they'd erected a permanent block after our first skirmish in the Rait Castle courtyard.

Abria had almost died that night when the Cait tossed her through a portal squarely into Underhill before I'd instructed the land to accept her presence. Roya had smothered her with magic long enough to hold life in her body until I found them.

Weariness washed through me. Poor Roya. She'd been caught up in a clan war. Because she was a changeling, she'd fallen in love with the son of a rival clan, who was also one of my creations. Sidhe blood sings to its own, no way around it.

Roya's father had plotted to murder her lover. She overheard the plans and warned him, but her father found out and sawed off her hands while she hung from one of Rait Castle's upstairs windows. I've never known what became of my other changeling. We located his body, but nothing magical remained. I've always suspected he switched forms before the human one breathed its last.

Roya still mourned him, so it was a safe bet he'd never returned to her arms. Perhaps the love had been one-sided, or at least lopsided where she'd cared more than him. Another thing I'd never know.

Wrenching my attention back to the task at hand, I laid both hands on the crystal orb. It warmed immediately and began to hum.

"Hush," I whispered.

Obligingly, it exchanged sound for a soft yellow glow. Trading my earth eyes for my third eye, I ran possibilities through my head. The Cait might be canny, but they were also lazy. The most likely spot for them was right under my nose. After a couple of settling breaths, I let a line tuned to Cait frequency resonate between my hands and the crystal.

Keeping my touch deft and sure, I pushed my magical senses in an arc. When my efforts yielded nothing, I widened my reach a little. Still nothing. Drawing back, I tested to make sure I was tuned to Cait-specific energy.

Check.

Had I been mistaken about them being close? I didn't believe so. Even if they were warded against my efforts, I should still be able to sense something. The crystal pulsed brighter, urging me to try once more.

Not too many "once mores" before I revealed myself. A glance over one shoulder showed Abria sitting on one chair with her feet propped on another. Hedrek perched on yet a third nearby. Her eyes were shut, but the owl was vigilant.

Arianrhod may have ordered the bird to watch out for Abria, but the goddess needn't have bothered. Anything with fur, fins, or feathers would have laid their lives down for Abria without any compunctions whatsoever.

Turning back to the crystal, I switched up where I touched it. The surface of the stone buzzed beneath my fingertips. Still taking care to be gentle, I tried a different approach. Instead of hunting for all Cait, I focused on one.

Labritha was the likely choice to take over once we'd killed the Cait's leader. Savage and unprincipled, she didn't waste time pretending to be anything other than what she was: a fierce warrior with blood in her eyes. She'd been one of the original Cait pressing for a schism between her people and the rest of the Sidhe.

My first scan was a repeat of what I'd done earlier. I'd been so tense, I was holding my breath. Sucking air softly, I sharpened the focus unique to my third eye.

And drew back fast. She was close to where I'd expected. Like as not, the rest of her kinsmen were with her. Had she felt my probing? Keeping my palms on the crystal, I waited, alert for any jab of power aimed my way.

The orb waited with me, pulsing waves of light almost as if it were breathing. A minute slipped past followed by another and then one more. Ten minutes later, I severed my connection with the orb and rocked back on my heels confident I'd pulled this off.

The Cait were on a small island in the Southern Ocean northeast of Australia, but south of the Kingman Reef. I was grateful they hadn't selected an off-world location. It would have made staging more difficult but not impossible.

I crossed the room to where Abria snored softly, draped between two chairs. *"Do you wish to come to my chambers?"* I asked Hedrek.

"Nay. I will hunt." Rather than doing anything as prosaic as spreading his great wings, the owl vanished in a flare of coppery sparks.

Tucking an arm under Abria's legs and another beneath her shoulders, I lifted her easily and rode a flow of magical currents through Underhill to my rooms.

"Did you find them?" Her voice slurred with exhaustion.

Familiar walls closed around us. With her still clasped in my arms, I strode to the bedroom and laid her on my rumpled bed. I'd left in a rush and hadn't taken time to straighten the duvet.

"Blake?" She sounded more awake this time.

I sat next to her. "Aye, I located them, but we have a bit of time. Would you like something to eat before you sleep?"

She nodded. By the time I returned carrying a tray with soup, bread, and wine, she'd fallen back asleep. Lying on her side with her red hair scattered around her, she looked young, carefree. The lines in her forehead and around her eyes had softened.

I placed the food on a table and sat on the floor to lever my boots off, intending to join her in a nap. Before I finished with the first boot, she was off the bed and staggering to the table. "Looks yummy," she murmured and picked up a soup bowl, drinking hungrily. Eventually, she sank into a chair.

I buttered bread, took the other chair, and we ate in silence.

"Would you like anything else?" I eyed the empty dishes.

"No. That was perfect. Have you thought more about Roya?"

"Not really. She was step two once I located the Cait."

Abria nodded. "I had a thought. Maybe we should put off tomorrow's mating ceremony."

I drew back. "Why? Did you change your mind?"

Alarm must have cascaded off me because she left her chair, sat in my lap, and twined her arms around me. "Of course not. But once we're mated, doesn't something magical in me shift? Make me more readily identifiable as Sidhe-linked?"

"Aye." I paused catching her meaning. "You're still determined to go with the cats. And maybe Roya."

"Yeah, I am. Someone has to. They're not warriors."

"But the Cait will recognize you," I protested. "From that night at Rait Castle."

A small shrug. "Can't be helped. If Roya can pull off lying to them, I probably can too."

Something icy tracked down my spine. I didn't want Abria anywhere near the Cait, let alone talking with them.

"It makes sense," she went on. "With my calling as an animal mage and all. I can throw myself on their mercy, tell them I hope they can forgive me, but that I've had a lot of sleepless nights since that battle. They're the animal branch of the Sidhe. I'm an animal mage. We shouldn't be at odds."

Listening to her, I almost, almost believed her tale. And then I sensed compulsion woven into her words. "You'll have to do better than that," I growled.

"Better than what?" she asked sweetly.

"You know exactly what I mean. If you're going to spell your words, you have to be more subtle."

Her full mouth spread in a soft smile. "I've heard you're a good teacher."

"The best, but refining magic can take years."

"Aw crap." She clapped a hand over her mouth and switched to telepathy. I heard her tell Hedrek we were moving the mating ceremony, but I couldn't decipher his side of the conversation.

"What'd he say?" I asked.

"That the animals will show up anyway. Perhaps we'll need them to fight."

Not if I had anything to say about it. In my version, this battle would take place half a world away. I wrapped my arms around her waist. "Come to bed, sweetheart. We both need rest."

She arched russet brows and laughed. "Rest, is it?"

I chuckled. "Aye, and perhaps other things."

"In that case"—she ducked from beneath my embrace and padded to the bathroom door—"we need to clean up."

The last of her words were drowned by water running into my oversized marble tub. She was right about the cleaning up part. I could smell myself. Standing, I stripped off my clothes and followed her to the steamy bathroom with its inlaid ivory marble tiles grained in copper.

Regardless of the outcome with Roya, I was going with Abria and her cats. She'd argue against it, but my mind was made up. We'd design a stealth operation. Quick in. Quick out.

And then we'd annihilate the Cait Sidhe. It made me sad, like cutting off a part of me. In a way, it was, since I'm bound to protect all with Sidhe blood.

Not those who rise against us, an inner voice was firm.

The sight of Abria's lithe, leggy form submersed in water drove everything else from my thoughts. Already naked, I slid in behind her, warm water closing over us both. My weariness fled; my cock hardened in record time.

Later was good...for everything but the woman encased in my arms.

CHAPTER 11
ABRIA

We didn't do the most bang-up job getting clean. Suds and shampoo flew everywhere as we dabbed, rubbed, rinsed. The water turned dingy, so murky I'd have liked to drain the mess and start over with clean, but I wanted Blake more than perfection on the cleaning front.

Somehow we ended up lying on soft, fluffy sheepskins in front of a crackling fire. He must have lit it with magic because he never left my side. The flames cast shadows that played over the magnificent lines of his face and body. Blake was a knockout wearing his human glamour, but his true form was even more elegant. Silky skin stretched over slabs of muscle. Iridescent black wings tickled as he wrapped them around me.

I loved the wing part. They were sultry and alien and comforting all in one eldritch package. When I'd first met him—or more accurately the day he'd chased me down—those wings had been hidden behind a glamour. I'd been riding Becca, a unicorn masquerading as a horse, that day. Maybe because of her habitual glamour, she'd seen through his right away.

His persistence and high-handedness had annoyed me, but he'd saved my ass too. I hadn't fallen into bed with him out of gratitude, though. I might be pathetic, but I'm not that pathetic. Nope. I invited him home because the attraction boiling between us was too intoxicating to deny. No matter how many ways we made love, the ardor never cooled. It was why I'd finally told him he had to leave. I couldn't have a life—not the one I'd been accustomed to—and him. Not even close.

Silly of me. Blake is my fate. My destiny. Months of persistence paid off because I stopped pushing him away. His energy and his magic drew me like a lodestone, too powerful to be denied.

His lips kindled heat and need every place he touched my skin; and he was doing quite a thorough job not letting any real estate lie fallow. He tongued a trail across my shoulders, down my ribs, across my hips. My nipples puckered, aching for him to pay attention to them, but he circled those bits and returned to the hollow of my throat.

Guilt about wasting valuable time nagged in a distant part of my brain; I smothered it. I'd spent months—years—training my power. Surely I deserved a few stolen moments that weren't goal-directed.

I cupped the side of his face in my hand. Copper-gold skin stretched over pronounced cheekbones and a square chin. No stubble in Sidhe-land. No beards, either. "I missed you," I murmured.

"Good to hear." Twisting, he kissed my palm. Shivers of delight coursed up my arm.

"Thanks for hunting me down."

He made a face. "Pfft. Arianrhod did not make it easy."

"No. She wouldn't."

Blake nestled his face into my hand. Warmth from him sang to a primitive part of my soul. We'd always been this way from the very first time we tumbled into my bed after the battle at Rait Castle. So hungry for one another, nothing else mattered.

"Tell me. Did she hold you against your will?" His dark eyes bored into mine, seeking truth.

I shook my head. "The situation between us was... improving. Those first weeks were tough. I did consider leaving, but she had some things I needed."

"Did she?" His scrutiny sharpened.

"Hate to admit it, but yeah. Cailleach got to a point where she said I'd be better served by another teacher. I fought it, but she'd never lied to me about anything. It took, um, time before I truly appreciated the breadth of Arianrhod's power."

Talk about understatements I stopped to take a breath and also because I wasn't sure where to go next.

"You left something out," Blake observed.

He always knew.

Reaching around, I ran my nails down the curvature of his spine to his high, tight ass.

"Nice try. I still want to know."

"We can talk later." I pulled him against me, rewarded by the press of his erection against my belly.

"Aye, later and now too." Familiar magic circled me, reassured me I was safe here in Underhill. Blake would protect me with his life, with his magic, with all the power a Sidhe prince brought to bear.

"Not fair." I licked the hollow of a collarbone.

"Everything is fair." He circled his arms around me and drew me closer still.

"You're not going to give up, are you?"

"Never. The sooner you tell me, the sooner we can, um, move on to more pleasant pursuits."

A chuckle turned into a full-blown laugh. As if we could resist one another for long. Mirth rolled through me. It felt good after the last couple of months when I'd always been on my guard and one step away from hunting for a way out of Caer Sidi.

Wriggling out of his arms, I flipped into a cross-legged sit where I had an unimpeded view of his glorious body. "Not much to tell," I said. "Arianrhod and Ceridwen came to visit Cailleach. They'd discussed my future without input from me. It pissed me off. Ceridwen had that damned kettle. I swear, the thing follows her around like a deranged puppy.

"Anyway, they told me I had no choice about the next steps in my training, and then the three of them vanished. A week passed. Just when I was beginning to relax, certain they'd changed their minds, Cailleach returned and announced I was slated to go to Ariahrhod's domain. I gathered a few things and was gone with very little conversation between us."

"Do you suppose she felt guilty?" Blake arched a dark brow.

I shrugged. "Who knows. The journey was rough. I wasn't in the greatest shape when I got to Caer Sidi. Not sure what I was expecting, but what I got was the antithesis of a warm welcome. To say things between us were strained puts a kind spin on it.

"After a few weeks where she showed up in the morning with the day's assignment and then vanished till the following morning, we finally talked one night." That conversation still rankled, and I made a bitter face. "Apparently, every time she looked at me, she saw failure. Not exactly encouraging, but it did explain why she avoided me as much as possible."

I blew out a breath, aware of how tired I was. "I'd seriously been considering leaving, letting you orchestrate whatever training I still needed, but something shifted after that evening. She was present more—and she found Hedrek for me."

Blake nodded. "She cares more than you think she does. I saw it in her eyes."

I grinned crookedly. "Yeah, I grow on people."

He mock swatted me. "Hussy."

"You want hussy? I'll show you hussy. Roll over."

Blake laughed, rich, deep, seductive. And rolled onto his stomach.

I grabbed a hip and tugged. "Not that way."

"Be specific, wench." His voice was muffled in the crook of an elbow.

Switching tactics, I straddled his waist, seating my core

over his deliciously naked flesh. Slow, deliberate, I bent until my mouth hovered over his shoulder blades and breathed on him. Just breathing, not touching, I moved in small circles from left to right and back to center.

He groaned but held still all except for his wings. They twitched.

After a few more breathing passes along his upper back, I slid lower until I was perched over the curves of his ass. Most of the moisture in my body had fled south, and I left a trail of desire in my wake, the musky scent a dead giveaway that I was deep in rut. I ran a single nail down the center of his back, keeping it centered on his spine. Next, I bent and followed it with kisses.

Another groan, this one louder, more fraught with need, told me he was struggling to hold his position. I slid farther still until I was midway down his thighs. Grabbing his buttocks with both hands, I opened them until the puckery bud of his anus was visible.

I traced a line to his scrotum. His balls were tense, snugged against his body. Backtracking, I teased his back door with a fingertip and kept slight pressure on his balls, all the while rocking back and forth to keep the most sensitive portion of me in contact with the backs of his thighs. Edging sideways, I straddled a leg to improve my connection.

My breathing had grown ragged. Heat spilled through me. Other than our brief dalliance in Caer Sidi, it had been months since we'd been together. This was turning into a contest of who could hold out the longest. My legs spread wider of their own accord to maximize the pressure of my clit against him. Not only could I come this way, it was torture to hold back.

What began as subtle thrusting turned hotter, more desperate. No longer just my fingertip, the whole digit was buried in his ass. His muscles clutched and released as his hips developed a rhythm. Moans and gasps told me he had his own set of struggles hanging on.

"Ready to turn over yet?" I panted.

"Thought you'd never ask." With a single fluid motion—and a magical assist—he flipped over, caught me from where I was suspended midair, and buried his cock inside my body.

Huge, hot, hard, he stretched me, filled me, completed me. Nothing fancy or subtle here. My nipples had turned to aching points of need. My nether regions were awash in lust. He held onto my waist and drove into me. Neither of us lasted beyond a dozen strokes.

A feral grunting filled the air. It didn't sound anything like me, but it was me sure enough as a climax ripped through my soul, spun me around, and spit me out. Maybe because I'd been deprived so long, another followed on its heels. Between the two, Blake released inside me. Long, lazy swoops of semen painted my vault. His hands dug into my sides, and his neck was tossed back, corded with passion as ecstasy took him.

Gasping, panting, we ground our bodies together trying to be closer still.

When straddling him required too much effort, I lay on

top of him with his arms and wings cradling me and his cock still buried in my body. We fell asleep like that, too done in for words or for more lovemaking.

Given what we'd been through, that we'd managed this much was a surprise.

BECAUSE UNDERHILL LACKS DEFINED day-night cycles, it was impossible to tell how long we drowsed against one another. When I opened my eyes, we were on our sides. Blake was supported on one elbow watching me, his dark eyes brimming with concern.

"What?" I murmured, my voice muzzy with sleep.

"Nothing. I just like to watch you."

"Don't lie to me, Blake." My tone was sharper than I'd meant it to be, probably because I wasn't fully awake.

"The part about liking to watch you is true," he protested.

"Sure, but that's not all of it."

"All right, but fair warning. You won't like what I came up with."

The last vestiges of sleep fled. My mini break from duty was over. Why did I have to be hunted? At the center of an eons-long vendetta blaming me for cracks in people's magical ability.

"Abria?" Blake's tone was so tender it drilled through my anger—and my pity party. He drew me against him.

I scootched deeper into his embrace, hoping to shut out the world. "It's okay. Go ahead and tell me."

"I'm coming along on the reconnaissance mission with you and your cats and maybe Roya."

He was right about one thing. I didn't like his suggestion. Except it was more like an edict. Suggestions could be ignored. No one should have to face danger because of me. It was bad enough the Cait had targeted their erstwhile kinsmen on my account.

"If I hadn't insisted on watching over my cats—the ones I have yet to recruit—would you still tag along?"

He stiffened against me. Perhaps he resented the term *tag along*. It gave me all the answer I needed. I disentangled myself and sat up. "If our positions were reversed," I said slowly, "and the lives on the line were Sidhe, would you abandon them to whatever happened?"

"I've sent many Sidhe into battle without feeling the need to watch over them," he replied. His voice had turned cool, neutral.

"That's because they're trained warriors," I retorted, oblivious to mixing metaphors and twisting facts to meet my needs.

"And your cats are not," he agreed. "I understand why you feel responsible, but I don't have to like it."

"It will be far more difficult to hide your energy and my own," I pointed out.

"Aye, but I'm not changing my mind." Blake hesitated. "We need Roya for my plan to be viable. If things unfold as I expect, the Cait will be so focused on her, they'll not be paying enough attention to discover you or me. Besides, none of us will be there long."

You hope. I kept that thought private. At the end of the

day, Cait are cats, and cats are skittish bastards who don't trust readily.

"Is there any reason for Roya to help out?" I asked. "Seems like she's given up enough in the service of the Sidhe. Changeling means you stole her when she was a human child, right? So, she lost her family on account of you."

A corner of his mouth curled into what could have been the beginnings of a hiss before he said, "And gained immortality."

"Whatever she had for family are probably long dead. Did you ever ask her if she saw immortality as a fair trade—for anything?" The words gushed out before I had a chance to stop them. I flapped a hand his way. "Sorry. Ignore that. I have no right to tell you how to run your affairs."

He was on his feet, facing away from me as he plucked garments out of a wooden chest. I needed something clean too. Maybe there was a storeroom here I could filch something from. And then I remembered my valise. Arianrhod had given it to me. Where had I left it?

When Blake turned around, he'd donned dark linen trousers, a cream-colored linen shirt, and a leather vest. He spread his hands in front of him. "I've done a lot of things I'm not proud of, but I've always put Sidhe needs first. In doing so, I've harmed others. I can't go back, Abria. Only forward."

My mouth fell open. It was so not the response I'd expected.

He crossed the room and extended a hand. I took it, and

he drew me to my feet. "Love the view, but you might want to get dressed. The clothes you wore yesterday are clean." He gestured behind him to an untidy stack on a table. "And your valise is in my sitting room."

I didn't bother to ask how—or when—either of those small miracles had occurred. While I was dragging on my pants, he said, "I'm going to the *Dreaming* to talk with Roya. No pressure. If she helps it will be because she wants to."

"Ditto for the cats I recruit."

He hugged me from behind, nuzzled my neck, and was gone in a flash of familiar magic leaving me alone in his rooms. I finished dressing quickly. Blake and I have had some doozies of arguments. That this one was over so quickly heartened me.

He's still coming along, an inner voice observed.

True, but some beaches weren't worth dying on. I'd appreciate his support on the one hand. One the other, if anything happened to him, I'd never forgive myself. Reality slapped me hard. He felt the exact same way about me. Ergo, his insistence I didn't enter the Cait stronghold alone.

After grabbing my shoes, I perched on the edge of the rumpled bed to don them and my stockings. The linens smelled of passion; I inhaled deeply once and then once more. My nether regions stirred to life. Good thing Blake wasn't here or we'd end up right back in bed.

I chuckled softly. As problems went, there were worse ones to have, but we'd never moved beyond the can't-keep-your-hands-off-me phase, and I doubted we ever would.

On my feet once more, I walked into the sitting room.

True to Blake's words, the rucksack I'd brought from Caer Sidi sat on a chair. I didn't remember dragging it in here, but it had followed me—or Blake had made certain it remained by my side. Not that it mattered. Nothing in it I needed.

I crossed the room, intent on leaving Underhill to hunt for potential recruits. The door flew open. Breanne's nostrils twitched, but she didn't make a snide comment about the apartment smelling like a bordello. Instead, she asked, "Where's Elwyn?"

I still wasn't used to hearing Blake's given name, but the Sidhe frequently called him by it. "He left."

"I can see that, child. I'm not blind."

Before she could retreat to two syllable words with spaces in between, I said, "He's in the *Dreaming*."

"What's he doing there?" Something I couldn't quit interpret lay beneath her question.

"Hunting for Roya."

Breanne huffed out a breath. "That cursed changeling. Whatever does he want with her?"

"You really need to ask him that." I was done being polite and listening to veiled criticisms.

"Don't get all huffy on me," she snapped. "You have visitors. Normally, I don't allow outsiders into Underhill, but Hedrek was with them." Her lips thinned into a tight line. "For some reason, Underhill recognized him and allowed him entry."

"He's already been here," I reminded her. "And he carries Arianrhod's mark."

"Pfft. Not much love lost betwixt us and the Celts."

"Where are my visitors?" I tried to sweep past her, but she blocked my way.

"In a small dining room."

"Where is it? I'm not all that familiar with your realm."

Hoots preceded Hedrek as he swept through the open door. "There you are." He circled Breanne. "You said you'd bring her to us."

She settled her hands on substantial hips. "I do not work for you."

"Then you shouldn't have offered to fetch Abria."

I smothered the grin that wanted out, and an inane desire to clap. Go Hedrek. Not much intimidated him, certainly none of the Celts.

Breanne's beefy cheeks sported red blotches. Spinning, she trudged from the room. Hedrek lit on my right shoulder, talons digging deep. "You might want to avoid alienating our hosts," I murmured.

"What about them alienating me?" he countered. "I arrived with a dozen animals intent on finding you. Before I got twenty meters into Underhill, a greeting party diverted us to a dingy, windowless space." He squawked in annoyance. "No food. No water. What kind of hospitality is that?"

"Not much at all," I agreed. "But in their eyes, no one measures up to their magic."

"Even if it were true—and it's not—it's no excuse for being rude. Come on. I'll guide you to the others."

I walked beneath the lintel and shut the door behind me. A jab of Blake's magic told me some type of indwelling warding jumped into play whenever the doors were shut.

Could I get back inside without him? I'd find out, but not just now.

The small dining room wasn't far. When I opened the door, three wolves, a couple of mountain lions, deer, goats, and raccoons were jammed into the space. They leapt for me yipping and purring.

"We came for your mating ceremony." A black wolf nudged me with his cold, wet nose.

"But then we found out it wasn't happening," a soft-eyed doe cut in. "What happened, dearie? Did you change your mind?"

"Not at all." I glanced at the press of bodies. "Let's continue this conversation outside where you can hunt and all of us can breathe."

Once, I'd have had to pick and stumble my way to an entry point. No more. With my augmented power, I draped a travel spell over all of us, visualized the Rait Castle court-yard, and moved us as a group.

"Oooh. You're stronger," the doe said.

"It explains her long absence." Hedrek stood up for me.

For once, sunlight streamed from clear skies. The grassy ground was still wet and muddy, but full of the scents of life and growing things. I perched on a flat rock. The animals ranged around me. Their devotion resonated in my soul; gratitude spilled through me.

I might be a one-of-a-kind mage, but it was the only kind I'd ever want to be.

Because I owed my friends an explanation—and because they'd spread the information through the rest of their kin—I told them about the Cait and the task at hand.

And reassured them Blake and I would be mated soon.

"Will we be welcome?" a wolf woofed.

"I want all of you there," I replied firmly. "We'll plan to do this outside, so you feel welcome. I'm sure Blake will agree."

Even if he didn't, I'd talk him into it. I had a feeling he'd want the pomp and ceremony of their infernal council chamber, but it wasn't big enough for all the guests I envisioned.

I clapped my hands together and exclaimed, "I've got it. We'll have the ceremony on the same beach where I first met Cailleach. That way the sea folk can be part of it too."

"Let us know when," a mountain lioness purred. When I looked closer, her belly was distended with yet-to-be-born young.

"I'll give you all the notice I can, but now I need to run down a few cats to help spy on the Cait."

"We're cats," the lioness said huffily, whiskers twitching.

"And amazing, wonderful ones," I agreed. "But the Cait look more like housecats in their animal bodies. You'd frighten them."

She looked pleased by the compliment. I slipped away, intent on my old neighborhood in Nairn. May as well hit up cats who knew me. They'd be more likely to help even after I outlined just how dangerous it would be. Hedrek stuck to me like glue.

"You'll have to conceal yourself," I told him before my spell spit us out in a deserted alleyway.

"All the thanks I get," he groused, but he understood. No

normal owl looked like him, and he'd draw unwanted attention when what I needed was stealth. Hopefully, I'd be done before one of my erstwhile neighbors noticed me and hustled over to find out where I'd been.

"I am grateful," I told the owl. "Now let's get this choo-choo heading down the tracks."

CHAPTER 12

BLAKE

Abria hadn't been as put out as I anticipated when I told her I planned on accompanying her. I wasn't going to bring it up until the last minute—when it would have been much harder for her to stomp all over my Sir Galahad behavior—but she'd caught me dead to rights when I was studying her as she slept. I could have evaded her question, but she'd have known I wasn't being straightforward.

I refused to lie to her, no matter how unpleasant the consequences.

I'd changed into clean clothes, but the scents of our lovemaking clung to my skin and tantalized my nostrils every time I inhaled. Leaving her in my chambers had been torture, not because I didn't trust her but because I wanted to remain by her side.

If I had my druthers, we'd never be separated. Also an unrealistic expectation. I'd never had this reaction to any woman before—and more than a few were scattered through my idle youth and adult years. I could walk away from them, but never from her.

I'd tried, albeit not very hard, when she booted me out of her flat. Only a couple of weeks passed before I began shadowing her, taking care she never knew. Embarrassment filled me. I wasn't much better than a common stalker, but my intentions had been far more pure.

When I'd finally shown myself and clarified my intentions, she'd been angry. Still, a tiny part of her had been glad to see me. I manipulated that part shamelessly—and then she'd left with Cailleach.

The diaphanous walls of the *Dreaming* formed around me. It's a sub-world to Faerie and Underhill. The only ones who can breach its boundaries are Sidhe and Fae.

Sometimes I'm surprised by whom I meet here. More often, I'm annoyed. The *Dreaming* is a neutral zone. No matter how badly one of my subjects has transgressed, once they reach the *Dreaming*, they're excused from punishment.

So long as they remain here.

The kicker is they cannot leave. There's no statute of limitations on crimes in my world. No judges or juries, either. I serve in both capacities. The council weighs in, but I have the final word. Not that Sidhe are inherently lawless. We aren't. But just like every society, we spawn the occasional rotter.

The soft, pulsing light of the *Dreaming* surrounded me. It's soothing and comforting and hypnotic. Centuries can pass here and feel like a mere handful of days. It's one of the reasons I never stay long. Not more than a month or two. I don't want to lose myself in its webbing. It would turn into a rerun of the Celts tripping me up with their Warcraft game.

I like to believe I'm immune, but I'm obviously not. The last time I'd bided here, I'd used it as a base to spy on Abria. Weak spots allow a clear view of Earth from several vantage points.

Since I didn't want anyone to know what I was about, I didn't call Roya's name. Neither did I employ magic to search for her. While it has many nooks and crannies, the *Dreaming* isn't all that big. Working systematically, I canvassed its corridors and chambers.

Just when I was wondering if she'd snuck away without me knowing—a distinct possibility—snatches of a song in her clear, pure alto reached me. She sang in Gaelic, and as I listened I realized she pined for her lost love. The other changeling I'd set to guard the gates to Underhill.

They hadn't known about one another, yet they'd been drawn together with disastrous consequences for them both. It was a harsh lesson, one reminding me not to meddle in mortals' affairs. The world has changed over the past few centuries. Magic takes a backseat to science these days, and stealing children for my own purposes is frowned upon. Back when I'd snatched Roya and Gillian, families never missed extra mouths to feed. In a backhanded way, I'd been convinced I was doing everyone a favor.

Talk about misguided, pigheaded, and blind to reality.

Following the string of haunting notes, I found Roya perched on a stack of colorful cushions cradling a songbird between her palms. The bird sang along with her in an evocative duet. Roya's long red hair hung in curls past her waist. Her chocolate eyes were almond-shaped and set above defined cheekbones. Still wraith thin, she was dressed in a flowing violet gown made of some silky material. Her feet were bare.

All in all, she looked far better than when I'd last seen her. Then her hair had been filthy and matted, her clothing naught but rags.

Her mouth stretched into a wide smile, and she bounded to her feet. Son of a bitch. She was actually glad to see me. If anyone had been the instrument of her misfortune, it was me. Guilt cut deep. After everything I'd done, I was about to ask for still more.

"Blake. What a lovely surprise." She reached me and held out arms that ended in stumps where hands had once been. The white songbird with a bright-red beak flapped to her shoulders.

I hugged her briefly and let go. "How have you been since the last battle?" I asked.

"Fine. No lasting ill effects." She cocked her head to one side and smiled. "How is Abria? She was actually injured."

"She made a full recovery. I'll tell her you asked."

"And the two of you?" Roya arched a red brow.

"We're planning a mating ceremony soon."

"Oooh, can I come? I'd love to see her again. She saved my life, what was left of it."

Guilt cut deeper still. Kind of Roya not to blame me for the wreckage.

Her smile faded. "Sorry, my liege. I overstepped, and—"

"Not at all." I placed a hand on her upper arm. "We'd

love to have you." I hesitated, gathering my thoughts. "I'm here to ask a boon."

"Anything, my liege."

I shook my head. "In this instance, I'm not your liege, and you are free to say no without any repercussions."

Her gaze bored into me, curiosity dancing in the depths of her eyes. Nothing to do but spit this out in as few words as I could manage.

"The Cait didn't give up. They're planning another offensive. We would be well-served if we had more information about their strategy and timing."

"Of course, but where do I come in?"

"At first, Abria thought to recruit a few cats. They'll pass relatively unnoticed in the Cait world. Then she announced she'd accompany them."

A furrow developed between Roya's brows, so I hurried on. "Since the Cait know you, it's logical for you to return to their midst. Tell them you've reconsidered. That the bastard of a Sidhe prince locked you in the *Dreaming*, and you escaped at great risk."

Roya closed her teeth over her lower lip. "It's an interesting approach, but they'll never believe me. They knew how much I hated them."

"Aye, but they're also arrogant. They just might believe you had a change of heart when faced with the reality of Underhill—or the *Dreaming*—and my kinsmen.

"You are under absolutely zero obligation to do this," I reminded her. "But if you showed up at their gateway with a few of Abria's cats in tow, I bet they'd let you in. They're deep in battle strategy. Extra bodies are always welcome."

"Pfft." She flapped a hand. "You mean extra cannon fodder."

"You won't be there very long." I aimed for reassuring.

"How can you know? Last time, one of them ate me up alive and sustained himself by draining my magic."

"Abria and I will be there too."

Her eyes widened. She fell back a pace. "But they'll find you."

"Not if they're focused on you."

Roya pinched the bridge of her nose with a palm. "I don't know. Seems risky. What exactly am I supposed to find out?"

"Everything you can. At this point, we know less than nothing, so any information will be useful."

The songbird spread its wings and flew down the corridor I'd walked. Guess he wasn't enamored with my plan, either.

"How long do I have to think about it?"

"Not long. Either you leave with me today, or you're off the hook." I aimed for a light tone, lighter than I was feeling. She would be a perfect diversion, but I refused to pressure her. I'd done enough damage to her and her life track. If she acquiesced it would be because she chose to, not because I coerced her.

Roya cast a longing gaze around the small, oval chamber. A pallet lay against one wall. That, her stack of cushions, a chest, and a few scrolls constituted the sum total of her possessions. I thought about offering a few more creature comforts, but it might be construed as bribery. I did make myself a promise, though. If she came with Abria and me, I'd see to it she had whatever she wanted in the *Dreaming* or wherever she chose to live.

"I'll do it," she said so softly I wasn't certain I'd heard correctly.

"Are you certain?"

She shook her head. "How could I be? But I want to help. The Cait are a poor excuse for magic wielders. They lie and cheat and manipulate everything they can to their advantage."

Her words sounded a warning. "Can you bury how you feel so deep they'll never ferret it out of you?"

A crooked grin. "Aye. That I can do. I hated my father, Laird Cummings, and he never figured it out till the end."

"The Cait are smarter than your father."

"In some ways, yes. In others, no. I lived next to them for a long while as they did their damnedest to whittle through my defenses."

"Why didn't you call me sooner? I could have helped."

She shrugged. "I like to solve my own problems." Turning away, she rummaged through the chest near her sleeping pallet and withdrew a multicolored shawl. Tossing it over her shoulders, she faced me and said, "Ready."

Just like that.

She trusted me, and it made me feel like a piece of crap. Not because I didn't have her best interests at heart now, but because I'd been so laggard in that department before. The least I could do was not burden her with an untimely confession, so I gathered magic into a travel spell and aimed for Underhill.

Hopefully, Abria would be back, and we could craft our

final game plan. The sooner we got in and out of the Cait stronghold, the better I'd like it.

Roya stood quietly by my side.

"Thank you," I told her.

"No need. I'm part of you. You made me Sidhe, gave me immortality. How could I refuse you anything?"

"I'll keep you safe, Roya. No matter what it takes."

Trust shone from her dark eyes. I vowed to be worthy of it.

CHAPTER 13
ABRIA

I never can judge what time of day it will be on Earth when I leave Underhill. Fate was with me, though. Nighttime burbled around us. No moon. No stars. Just a bank of dark, scudding clouds and an icy drizzle. Maybe Hedrek was safe in his usual form. No one would be out and about in this weather unless they had urgent business.

Inverness has more than its share of crime. By contrast, Nairn is a sleepy little hamlet where they roll up the sidewalks at dusk. Night is also when cats like to prowl. Before I could look for them, they found me. Furry shapes converged from both ends of the alley meowing up a storm.

I sank into a crouch, held out my arms, and they dive-bombed me, hissing and spitting to hang onto my lap, a prime piece of real estate. Word traveled. Before long, over twenty cats surrounded me. I petted, stroked, and cooed, suddenly unwilling to risk any of their precious lives no matter how important the task.

Hedrek kept to the shadows. Even normal-sized owls are a threat to kittens and smaller cats. Somehow, he knew instinctively to shield his energy.

"Are you coming home?" a large black tomcat wanted to know. With matted fur and a torn ear that had never healed properly, he was a veteran of many squabbles.

A chorus of, *"Yes, home,"* followed his words.

I hesitated before answering. I could leave without upsetting their ranks with my request for aid. They'd never know the difference.

"Let them choose," rolled through my head from Hedrek weighing in.

"Choose what?" the black tomcat asked in out-loud speech. Cats have a hell of a time forming words, so they were garbled.

I cradled the cats in my lap before reaching out to touch others who sat nearby. "I came to ask your help," I began.

"Anything," the black tom said promptly.

I shook my head. "Wait until you hear everything before you volunteer. This will be dangerous. You might never return."

Purrs, meows, and hisses ground to a halt. Many sets of eyes stared at me. To not belabor the point, and to make certain I was clear, I stuck to the shortest version I could muster.

The Cait Sidhe had delusions of grandeur, of taking over the Sidhe. If that happened, the latitude extended to all creatures would be severely overhauled. "We must stop them," I continued. "It's where you could come in. The Cait have an affinity for all things feline. If you request asylum, they won't deny you."

"Asylum from what?" a calico female asked. Pink tongue swooshing out, she cleaned her whiskers with a paw.

"From the Sidhe who tried to imprison us," the large black tom inserted.

"But they didn't," the calico protested.

"If we're convincing, they'll believe us," the tomcat reassured her.

Aw crap, he was really getting into this, but it made sense. He lived for fights, except they took place in familiar territory. Rising from where I knelt on damp cobblestones, I said, "Hush. I need you to listen before you make any decisions."

They ranged before me, tails twitching, eyes glistening with enthusiasm. "The Cait stronghold is far from here. We would transport you there with magic. Once you've arrived, your task will be to talk your way inside." I stopped long enough to huff out a breath. "Shouldn't be all that difficult. The Cait are swayed by flattery. If you tell them some version of how you've always worshipped them, wanted to be part of their ranks, it should work."

"What happens after we're inside?" the calico meowed.

"Do not draw attention to yourselves, but listen as well as you're able. Any information about their plans is more than we have now. You won't want to be there long, and extricating you will be tricky."

"In what way?" The tomcat twitched his long whiskers.

"I'm going to assume their current location is arranged a lot like Underhill, which means it's guarded by the Cait or the land—or both. If they allow you entry, fine and well. But once there you won't be able to simply walk out. It's where Blake and I come in. And maybe Roya."

"Who's she?" the tomcat asked.

"A changeling bound to service by the Sidhe."

"Doesn't that mean they stole her away from her pack when she was little?" another cat asked.

I nodded. "Yeah, but she's worked with the Sidhe for centuries. Her loyalty is assured. She saved my life during a battle with the Cait—after I saved hers."

"How will you extract us?" the tomcat asked, circling back to what I'd been talking about.

"With magic, but it's not as simple as it sounds. If the Cait have even the slightest suspicion you're not what you claim, they'll eviscerate you on the spot. No judge. No jury. No questions."

After pausing to let my words sink in, I went on. "This is truly dangerous. I'm hoping for two volunteers, but I would understand if you chose not to go. Roya might be able to pull this off on her own. She has history with the Cait, history we're hoping to leverage."

"Are you certain she's coming?" The calico swished her tail.

"No, I'm not. And it will be far more difficult for you if she's not there."

"Only two of us?" another cat tossed at me.

My heart squeezed painfully in my chest. I didn't want to send any of them. "Only two," I reiterated. "I hate to even ask that because you'll do most anything for me."

"Give us a moment," the black tomcat said.

"Certainly. We'll wait at the head of the alley." Gesturing to Hedrek, I set a brisk pace for the street beyond to offer the cats privacy to talk among themselves. The leaden skies had partially cleared; the chill drizzle had lessened.

"For a minute there, I thought you changed your mind," the owl observed.

"For a minute there, I nearly did." We reached the junction of alley and boulevard, stopping just shy of where cobblestones turned to asphalt.

"This is everyone's war," Hedrek told me, hooting softly. "Their lives will change if the Cait take over both the ley lines and how power spills through them."

The damned ley lines. I still had that task ahead of me. The reconnaissance to Cait Sidhe-land was a blip on the radar screen. Necessary, but a sidebar to events that lay ahead. There might be a full-scale war between the Sidhe and their Cait cousins. It would damn near flatten Blake. He hadn't given up on his kinsmen seeing the light—or maybe he had, but their defection still broke his heart.

A thought frittered across my mind. What would happen if I addressed the ley lines first? Before any battle was fought. Could I alter the outcome if I repaired whatever damage my making had caused? I didn't see how. If power flowed more freely, it was bound to help both the Sidhe and the Cait. The only advantage I could identify was magic-wielders would stop hunting me.

Maybe. Old habits died hard.

Would I have time to track down the ley lines? Or would a battle ensue on the heels of our visit to the Cait? So many unknowns. My mind was mush as I worked to sort what I did know into a logical sequence.

Blake could help with that, but I didn't want to be dependent on him. For anything.

Hedrek flapped to my shoulders and perched there, feathers brushing the side of my face. "I will be there," he informed me.

Oh-oh. "There, where?"

"Wherever you are," the owl informed me. "Arianrhod tasked me with your safety."

A drunken couple staggered past a few feet ahead, craning their necks to identify the source of our voices. I switched to telepathy and cast a quick don't-look-here spell.

"No need for you to come when we visit the Cait," I informed him.

"Perhaps not, but I'll be there."

I twisted my head to glance up at him. *"The more of us, the greater the risk. I didn't want Blake along. He insisted."*

"Never turn your back on an ally."

"I'm not. It's just I'm used to working alone. I'm who takes the risks and deals with any consequences."

"That was your old life," Hedrek informed me.

My temper stirred to life; I batted it into submission. Now wasn't the time to throw a hissy fit. I had no "old life" to return to. Those doors had shut firmly behind me. If my ley line gambit failed, sooner or later the mob hunting me would be successful. They'd snuff me out, drain my magic, and walk away dusting their hands together certain they'd done all of magic-kind a favor.

Besides, I loved Blake. Walking away from him would leave a hole in my heart that would never heal.

That's what comes of letting people in, a sour inner voice spoke up.

Feline energy surged toward where I stood. I turned to face them and draped a hastily constructed sound shield around our end of the alley. In case some other late-night party-goers wandered down the street.

The black tom cat, clearly a spokesman for the group, stopped a meter from me, head and tail held high. "I am called Abel. Marika and I will accompany you," he said in formal tones.

"Are you certain?" I asked.

"We are," Marika, the calico who'd spoken earlier, joined Abel. "We understand the risks and accept them willingly."

My eyes stung with the quick hot bite of tears; my throat thickened. If they weren't bonded to me, they might not have agreed, but I couldn't go there. Before I tripped myself up overthinking things, I shaped a journey spell.

Prior to triggering it, I said, "Thank you for your devotion and trust in me."

Another cat padded forward. "If something...happens, you will return and tell us."

"Of course," I agreed. My voice developed a rough edge as I fought back a full-blown crying jag. It was so unlike me, but I didn't know what to do with the emotions coursing through my body. I wasn't in the habit of requesting help. Never mind help that could spell the end of my assistants.

Hedrek joined his magic to mine. We encompassed the two cats, and the alley fell away replaced by one of Underhill's many corridors. I was still working on getting my bearings—Underhill can be disorienting for the non-Sidhe of the world—when Blake and Roya found us.

The changeling barreled into me, hugging me tight. I returned her embrace. "Good to see you."

"You as well," she returned, still clinging to me. "And you look a hell of a lot better than last time."

"I could say the same about you." I gently disentangled my arms from her body. She was still thin, but clean and well kept.

Blake knelt before Abel and Marika and was thanking them warmly for being part of our mission. When he stood, he gathered them into his arms. "Come on," he said to Hedrek and me. "Food is laid out in one of the small dining rooms. We will eat, firm up our plans, and be gone."

"We'd rather hunt," Abel announced.

"No mice here," Blake told him. "Not much else edible that's on the hoof, either. Come see what's available. If it's not to your liking, you and Marika can hunt before we leave."

"Fair enough," the tomcat agreed.

I traipsed along corridors, following twists and turns. Either this was a part of Underhill I'd never seen, which was entirely possible, or the enchanted realm shifted and changed at will.

Finally, Blake turned beneath a curved lintel. He hadn't been kidding about food being laid out. Given there were only three of us, the owl, and two cats, he'd really overdone things.

"Raw is on that table." Blake gestured to his right.

Hedrek and the cats rushed to platters of dripping flesh.

I stopped by a teapot and poured a fragrant mix of herbs into a ceramic mug, followed by a splash of cream and a dollop of honey. Roya followed suit. I hovered a bit to see if she needed help, but she managed easily without hands. Of course, she'd had years of practice.

"Would you care for a splash of mead in that?" Blake asked.

Nodding, I held my cup out to him and then walked to the far side of the room. After placing bread, cheese, fruit, and roasted meat onto my plate, I dropped into the nearest chair.

I hadn't realized how hungry I was until I raised fork to mouth. After the first bite, I shoveled food with barely a pause to breathe. A glance at the cats and Hedrek suggested Blake had done well choice-wise. Both ate with single-minded purpose.

"Thank you for leaving the *Dreaming*," I said to Roya once my hunger had subsided, and my blood sugar was on its way up from ground zero.

"I'm recovered. Besides, there isn't much to do there. I weave. I sing. There is a bird who's become a friend."

"I'm sure you'd be welcome here," I began.

She shook her head. "Too many people. No one bothers me in the *Dreaming*."

"Until I did today," Blake murmured. Rising to his feet, he retrieved the mead bottle and poured the rich amber liquid into our cups. Next, he crossed to where the owl and cats were just finishing the raw meat.

"When you're done, join us so we can plan."

"Done now," Hedrek hooted and dipped his bloody beak in a conveniently placed bowl of water.

Abel and Marika dipped water to wet their paws, and then cleaned their snouts before gliding across the room.

"I've been thinking about this," Roya said once everyone sat in a circle with the tables behind us.

"Go on," Blake urged. "You'll be point person, so however we proceed has to resonate with you."

The skin around Roya's eyes developed a pinched aspect. "We'll know quickly if they fall for my story. I'll tell them I finally, finally crafted an escape from the *Dreaming*. You"—she pointed at Blake—"might be right behind me. I'm frightened, seeking asylum. No place else to turn to."

Abel yowled. "We came with you. We've always worshipped the Cait, wanted to be a part of them."

I tested their words and their resolve, searching for holes in their story. "Might work," I said thoughtfully. "Keep it short and sweet. Not too many explanations."

"Precisely," Blake weighed in. "A bigger problem will be concealing Abria and me."

"And me," the owl hooted.

Blake cast a sideways glance Hedrek's way. "Could you sit this one out, mate?"

The owl shook his head firmly.

"Arianrhod tasked him with my safety," I explained.

"Don't worry about me," the owl said. "I'll manage my own warding. Because my energy isn't what anyone is ever on the lookout for, my presence won't be our undoing."

Eh. Perhaps he had a point. "Where will we be?" I asked

Blake. "Inside the Cait Sidhe stronghold or beyond its gates?"

"We must be within," he replied. "Otherwise, we'll be too far away if something slews sideways."

I'd wondered if the Cait could bar all entry to their lands. The answer was probably yes since the Sidhe didn't have any trouble keeping unwanted folk out.

Blake let his gaze fall on each cat, the owl, and finally Roya. "This may not work, but I will attempt to maintain a faint link with each of you. If anything seems amiss, and I do mean anything, think the word Ceridwen. The moment I hear it, I'll break every rule to extricate everyone."

His stunning features hardened into menacing lines. "This is all or none, people. If one of us fears they've been exposed, we all leave regardless of whether or not we have the information we came for."

"What precisely are we looking for?" Abel asked.

"Anything you can glean about Cait plans to attack the other Sidhe," Roya told him.

"Or Cait plans period," I spoke up.

"Questions?" Blake's gaze made the rounds once again.

Roya nodded. "What if they ask how I found them?"

Blake frowned. "Glad you brought that up since I had to use my ancient bonding with all Sidhe to unearth their location."

I chewed my lower lip and finally said, "How about this? Roya held onto some residual bits of Cait essence from the time she spent subsumed by one. It was enough to allow her to track where they'd gone."

"Works for me," Roya said. "It will reveal my ability to

teleport, but it can't be helped since that's the only way I'd ever have crossed oceans to get to where they are now."

"Any more questions?" Blake inquired.

This time, no one had any. Judging from a shift in the emotions sloughing off everyone, the seriousness of our endeavor was just now sinking in.

"Where exactly are we going?" Roya asked. "Is it off world?"

"A small island in the Southern Ocean northeast of Australia," Blake told her. If it has a name, I haven't found it. I'll bring us out a respectable distance from the entry to their hideaway. Should be safe enough."

"Unless they've posted sentries," Hedrek cawed.

"We'll find out soon enough," Blake agreed. "One last thing. If fortune turns against us, my priority will be rescuing Abel and Marika. The rest of you can teleport. Once anyone even breathes Ceridwen, we're out of there. Do not wait for me to rescue you."

"How will the rest of us know?" Roya asked.

"Assuming my link remains intact, I'll speak the same word, Ceridwen. It's your cue to hightail it out of there anyway you can." He paused. "If you need me to finesse your escape, reach for me with your mind. We might exit in shifts, but I give you my word, I will not leave any of you behind."

"How can you be so sure?" Abel asked.

I had to hand it to him. Standing up to Blake took guts, even for me.

The Sidhe prince spread his black wings and transformed into what might have been his true body. I had no idea which form was primary, but I sure as hell hadn't seen this iteration. Suddenly, he was taller, broader, and far more intimidating. Power swirled around him in blues and violets.

"The Cait are still my subjects." His voice, deeper and harsher, echoed off the walls. "They must obey me, at least for a short time. It will give us the window we need to escape."

"Why for a short time? Why not forever?" Hedrek squawked.

"Because they can ward me out, but if they're not expecting my presence, it will take a while for them to erect a defense."

Blake was done talking. Sinking into himself, he once again looked familiar as he built a journey spell. Gesturing us close, he kindled it. Abel was in Roya's arms. Marika draped around her shoulders. Good idea, so they'd smell more like her than Blake or me.

All too soon, the darkness of our travel pod shattered. We stood in the midst of thick tropical vegetation; the salt scent of the sea lay thick in my nostrils. I stretched power, shielding it as best I could, and hunted for Cait energy. Breath hissed from between clenched teeth.

I was more nervous than I thought.

"It's that way," Roya said softly and struck off to the northwest with both cats.

I started after her, but Blake called me back. "Give them a chance to get inside," he said. "Then we'll teleport in and set up a vantage post."

"We have to be closer," I insisted. "What if they don't get

in? What if whoever shows up at the gates sees through them right away?"

"My links are live," he informed me.

"Even so, closer is better," Hedrek hooted and flapped skyward.

"Two against one"—Blake sported a crooked half grin—"is majority rule. Guess I've been outvoted."

Summoning magic to muffle my presence and any noise I made traipsing through tangled roots and noisy leaves, I set off. Blake took to the skies, flying behind the owl.

Another surprise. I hadn't realized the wings were other than decorative. Suppose I should have known better. The sound of voices reached me, faint and then loud enough to make out without deploying magic. I'd decided to use as little as possible to minimize my odds of discovery.

Roya went through the script she'd floated back at Underhill. It wasn't word for word, but close enough. A Cait —or maybe more than one—heard her out and told her to wait. I stopped, barely breathing. When I looked skyward, I couldn't locate Blake or the owl.

Time passed. The sun, which had been close to midheaven, dipped low in the western sky. I rocked quietly from foot to foot to keep them from falling asleep. Finally, I heard something like a gate creaking open and the words, "Come inside. We will grant you an audience."

I waited another hour after the last sounds had died away before making my way in their general direction. Before I came within sight of anything resembling a gate, Blake and Hedrek materialized, one on each side.

"I'll find my own way," Hedrek told us and flickered to motes of copper-colored light.

"Time to go inside," Blake said. The bite of his magic surrounded me, swathing me in layers of concealment. "Ready?"

I wasn't. Not really, but I nodded. The sooner we were inside the Cait fortress, the sooner we could launch our plan. Except, Roya had presumably already set that ball in play.

We traded jungle for cool dampness and the stench of cats, hundreds of them. Almost gagging on the reek of nonexistent hygiene, I marshaled my resources. What the hell? Cats were clean creatures. Why did their den smell worse than a pack of dung beetles?

Several sashayed within a meter of us. As soon as they left, Blake herded us to a small alcove. It seemed sightly removed from the traffic flow.

So far, so good. We were inside. All of us.

Now all we had to do was gather a bit of information and make good on our escape.

CHAPTER 14
BLAKE

I shielded Abria with magic and my body as I pushed us into the only halfway reasonable position near where we'd entered the Cait's realm. No one had noticed us so far, but if I moved around too much, it could jeopardize our mission.

This wasn't the most comfortable spot, but I wouldn't risk hunting for a better one. We might be here for hours. If our mission dragged on beyond a day or so, I'd reconsider. I'd been concerned the Cait would sniff us out. Not much risk of that. I couldn't believe how far they'd fallen. To live in the midst of such an unholy stench suggested they'd lost their minds.

Abria had killed their leader during the battle in Rait Castle's courtyard. I had no idea who'd taken over, but he should be ashamed. No Sidhe, fallen or otherwise, lived in such crude conditions.

Ever so gently, I tested my links to Roya, Abel, and

Marika, relieved they remained intact. I paid out a thread of magic to figure out where Hedrek was but thought better of it. The less enchantment I tossed about, the better.

Abria nudged me. When I glanced at her, she arched a brow. I shook my head and laid a finger over my mouth. Telepathy requires a trickle of power. Better for us to remain silent unless a good reason to do otherwise reared its head.

Time passed. I sank into a crouch, back leaning against a dirt wall. Abria did the same. We remained like that, shoulder to shoulder. The occasional Cait hustled past, sometimes in cat and sometimes in human form. I caught snatches of conversation, but they never amounted to much.

Did I dare eavesdrop through my connection with Roya?

I considered the option. It held appeal because it would offer a heads up if I needed to intervene and move her and the cats out of this place. But strengthening my link, a prerequisite to listening in, would also up the odds of discovery.

"It's been hours." Abria's mind voice was low, muted, worried.

"Could well be hours more."

"Are you certain they're all right?"

I made a chopping motion with one hand and placed my mouth right over her ear. No Cait had passed anywhere near us for a long while, so the odds of being overheard were thin. "If they weren't," I whispered, "Roya would have used the pull-the-plug word."

"This is hard. I want to do something." Her voice was so low I had to strain to hear her.

A cacophony of yowls and hisses snapped my head

around. The empty walkway filled with cats all rushing deeper into the fortress. Something was definitely up. I pushed to my feet and offered Abria a hand. Waiting until the last Cait ran past, we fell in behind them.

To hell with our safe little cocoon. If Roya's ruse had been discovered, I needed to be there to ensure her escape. Abria kept pace, clearly relieved we weren't still sitting around on our asses. Ordering her to retreat, remain where we'd been, was a waste of breath. She'd defy me, and we couldn't afford to waste energy arguing.

Corridors bisected others in a regular warren of passage-ways. Occasionally, the salt smell of the nearby ocean cut through the rancid reek of cat shit, cat piss, and cat puke. Someone had cleared most of the stones aside, but the walls were still studded with limestone, turquoise, and garnets. Moisture dripped from the ceiling in spots, suggesting we were closer to the surface than I'd thought.

As I ran, I reached for Earth's presence beneath our feet, not sure what to expect. All Sidhe carry a strong bond with the natural world. In Underhill, Earth recognizes me as sovereign. Here, she was troubled, agitated. I soothed her as best I could, but nothing shy of dumping the Cait off this bit of real estate would do.

Not wanting to extend hollow promises, I said I'd attempt to help.

A low, rounded side corridor forced me to hunch. Surely, the Cait hadn't excavated this cave system. My bet was it had once been a nesting ground for seals or sea lions. Marine birds probably used it to move their nests out of the weather.

Had the Cait kicked the former occupants out? If so, where had they gone?

I hesitated at every choice point until the sound of raised voices made my directional choices obvious. Abria grabbed my arm and pointed to a declination between two large rocks not unlike the spot we'd left.

We folded into it about the time Roya's voice separated from the dissonance streaming from what was probably a meeting hall dead ahead.

"You've asked me this same set of questions twice before," she was saying. "Either believe me, and let's get on with business, or I'm leaving."

"You're not going anywhere," a voice boomed.

Try as I might, I couldn't identify the speaker. Not without a judicious splat of power.

"Then kill me and get it over with. Not as if you didn't try for years."

Outraged yowls from Abel and Marika punctuated her words and made it clear they'd fight to the death for her.

"We came in good faith," Marika said. I could just imaging her puffing up her neck muff.

"Aye, we have always idolized you," Abel cut in.

"Seems we made a mistake," Marika snarled.

"Tell us why you're here," the voice I couldn't identify demanded.

"Last time I'm doing this, so listen up," Roya replied with just the right edge of defiance. "I heard rumors in the *Dreaming* about an imminent attack. The Sidhe had no right to imprison me. I've done naught but good for them since they ripped me from my family years ago."

"Not looking like you were very 'imprisoned,'" the voice went on.

"I escaped."

"Why now and not before?" another voice chimed in.

A sharp noise that might have been Roya stamping a foot or clapping her stumps together filled my ears. "You will treat me with respect," Roya announced. "If you do not, we've naught to talk about."

Good for her. The changeling had backbone. Maybe I hadn't done her as raw a turn as I thought.

Or maybe she grew strong because she had to, one of my wiser inner voices commented.

A slight ripple next to me served as notice the owl had joined us. I couldn't see him, but a dribble of his essence leaked through before he cut its flow.

"Wait outside this chamber," someone instructed.

"What's to stop me from walking out of here?" Roya inquired sweetly.

"You'll never find your way. The halls are spelled against intruders."

I bit back a laugh. Not spelled very effectively since nothing had slowed us down. Beneath my feet, a slight rocking suggested Earth had something to do with our successful transit of the Cait's domain.

Roya had said walk. Perhaps the Cait weren't worried about magical means of travel. If she raised power to escape via teleporting, they'd sense it and stop her. Or try to. As stinky and wretched as these caves were, I had my doubts their magic was up to snuff.

Good bit of data to file away.

Boot heels thudded on packed earth. Roya strode into the corridor with Marika in her arms and Abel wrapped around her shoulders. I tightened our warding. No percentage to her knowing we stood three meters away. It wasn't as if we could talk without alerting the Cait's attention.

The Cait. Aye, I needed to hear what they said. If the vote—and I felt certain they'd cast one—went against Roya, we'd have to get her out of here pronto. Making certain Abria was fully encased in concealment spells, I gathered my part of the enchantment and glided soundlessly toward the chamber entry looming ahead.

Familiar faces stood in lines facing a long, raised table at the far end of a large hall. They'd erected a sound shield, but I drilled through it and placed an ear next to the hole.

It appeared Zottre, not Labritha, had picked up the reins of leadership. In his human form today, his pale hair was braided close to his head. His brows formed question marks. His chin was pointed, as were his ears. Amber eyes with vertical slit pupils sat above slanted cheekbones. "We need extra bodies," he was saying. "Do any here disbelieve her enough to condemn her?"

"Wonder if those cats have kinsmen who would help?" Catrina mused. Silver-gray hair fell down her back in ripples. She shared the same sharp features as the other Cait, with moss-green eyes and thin lips.

All the Cait were naked. It made sense. Shifting forms was simpler if you didn't have to disrobe first.

"The cats and their kinsmen are secondary," Zottre redirected Catrina before raising his arms above his head. "All in favor of admitting Roya to our ranks, raise your hands."

I waited, so intent on what would happen next I barely missed two late-to-arrive Cait. They'd have run right into me if I hadn't scrambled aside.

I faded back toward where I'd left Abria and Hedrek, all the while shaping power into a journey spell while trying to be subtle. Another pitching roll beneath my feet served as a reminder Roya wasn't the only one counting on me. I released my nascent casting.

If we had to extricate Roya and the cats quickly, I'd leave it to Abria and Hedrek. Remaining behind, I'd do what I could to assuage our Mother Earth.

"Roya. Step forward," Zottre called.

She marched into the chamber, head high.

"The vote has been tallied," Zottre informed her. "You may remain in our midst, but you must also fight for us."

"Wouldn't have it any other way," Roya replied, her voice low and musical.

Relief swooshed through me. We were in. After a couple of all-Cait meetings, we'd have enough information to leave. I hoped. Zottre must have dismantled the sound warding to call Roya back and then resurrected it because I couldn't hear anything further.

There'd never be a better time to find a more viable hiding place. All the Cait were in the meeting hall. No more stragglers had appeared. I didn't dare use power to muffle my steps, so I moved as silently as possible in the direction we'd come with Abria and the owl flanking me. As I walked,

I scouted each branching hallway until I found what I sought.

One headed deeper into hillside. It didn't smell of cats, suggesting the Cait never used this particular part of the cave system. A hundred meters in, the passage opened into a small oblong chamber with a spring in its center. Fresh water was precious in oceanic environments, but the Cait had missed this one.

Retreating partway along the corridor, I sealed it with inward-turning wards. After testing their integrity, I was satisfied they'd conceal us over the short haul. When I returned to the spring, Abria and Hedrek were drinking.

"Can we talk?" Abria asked.

I nodded.

"Even if the Cait reveal plans in front of Roya, they'll change them up once she vanishes," Abria said.

"Maybe not," Hedrek hooted. "Depends how she leaves."

"What do you mean?" I asked the owl.

"She will need to travel with them and only drop out after the battle begins."

"Roya doesn't know that," Abria protested.

"We'll have to find a way to tell her," I muttered. Earlier, I'd been close enough to touch her. Surely, I could manage that again. "Remain here," I told the others.

"Where are you going?" Abria asked.

"To talk with Roya."

"But how? It's not safe. You could blow her cover."

"Trust him," Hedrek crooned amidst Abria's grumbling.

I could have hugged the owl. Instead, I gambled a quick teleport to the far side of my barrier, taking care to remain in the unused corridor. When Cait didn't rush out of every nook and cranny, I amped up my warding and hustled back the way we'd come.

I had to punch a new hole in the sound shield before I ascertained the meeting was still going strong. No one was paying the slightest attention to Roya. She and the cats stood off to one side behind several circles of Cait Sidhe.

There'd never be a better time.

"Roya." I breathed her name in mind speech.

"Aye?" She didn't look up, didn't switch positions that I could tell. Hell, she didn't even twitch.

"You must remain with the Cait until the battle begins. I'll be nearby." I thought about adding not to worry, but I was already pushing it. So far, no one had jerked an ear or a whisker in my direction.

"Already figured that part out."

She didn't require a pep talk. I'd said all I needed to. On my way back to where I'd left Abria and Hedrek, familiar power surged around me. The Earth. Before I could protest, tell her I was working on her problem too, a whoosh of chilly air tumbled me down a chute I hadn't seen. Probably because it hadn't been there.

I fell a long way before the bottom rose up to meet me.

"Fix this." Earth's multi-tonal voice grated. Listening to her reminded me of rockfall mixed with waves crashing on a barren shore.

After scrambling upright, I scanned yet another cave, this one littered with stalagmites, but didn't see the goddess. I spread my hands in front of me. "What would you have me do?"

"Make them leave. They're your minions."

In her world, sure. In mine, not so simple. "Soon they will march on us," I told her. "We will do our best to ensure none return here."

"What do you mean march on you? They're part of you." She sounded put out.

"They were part of us," I corrected her. "They left, and now they fight us."

"Ugh. Why couldn't you keep control of your own?"

It was a good question, but I lacked an answer. Instead, I started to reassure her of my good intentions. Before I could, the same blast of air that had moved me here deposited me in the corridor above.

A Cait, probably a messenger, barreled into me. Since I was invisible, he looked baffled and searched the ground for what he'd tripped over. I could have drained his essence. Instead, I reached inside his mind, erased the last sixty seconds, and hoped to hell I wouldn't regret my clemency.

The Cait hurried on his way, oblivious.

If the other Cait were on their toes, they'd sense remnants of alien power—mine—clinging to their own. Then again, maybe they wouldn't be on the lookout for anything. Nothing like planning an insurrection to provide a distraction.

The dice were cast. I couldn't undo my actions. Killing him would have been a dead giveaway. Even if I'd gotten rid of the body, vestiges of his misery would have lingered. Moving quickly, I located the path to Abria and Hedrek, hopped through my barrier, and ran lightly toward the chamber.

Before I reached it, the dirt under my feet rolled alarmingly. Once, and then again. Crap. Was Earth taking matters into her own hands?

The next few minutes would tell that tale. If I'd known she was on the verge of launching her own solution, I'd have done a better job coordinating our efforts.

CHAPTER 15
ABRIA

Despite Hedrek's reassurances, I paced from one end of the chamber to the other, neatly avoiding the spring. How could the Cait have missed this spot? None too much water in these caves that I'd noticed. Yet, this particular spot didn't smell of cats. Was it hidden from them in some inexplicable fashion? Seemed unlikely.

"Maybe it's a trap," I muttered.

"It's not," the owl retorted.

"But how can you know for sure?"

Hedrek flapped to my shoulders, talons digging deep. "Have you ever met a patient cat?"

"They can be patient while hunting." I felt oddly defensive of anything animal linked. Even if the Cait had targeted me, they were still similar enough to cats that worshipped me to engender protectiveness. Stupid of me, but there it was.

"They don't deserve anything from you," Hedrek squawked.

"Neither here nor there. How do you know we didn't walk into a trap?"

"Because they'd have sprung it," the bird announced.

"Maybe they have no idea we're here," I argued. "They're all engrossed in the meeting where Roya, Abel, and Marika's futures are being determined."

"They're not dimwitted," Hedrek shot back. "If they went to the trouble to boobytrap this spot, they'd have an automatic monitoring system in place. Think about it. Setting any kind of magical snare requires an ongoing output of power to keep it active. No one would do that without adding a silent sentry."

I focused inward. We'd been here at least half an hour, perhaps as much as forty-five minutes. A long span in magicdom. "Maybe you're right," I mumbled.

"You know I am." After a final painful squeeze with his talons, the owl jumped down.

Even absent this cavern being dangerous, I was worried about Blake. Should I go after him? Would it compromise our position to have two of us wandering around? My brain and my gut were at odds. If I listened to the former, I'd stay put. The latter screamed to go after him. What if our cover was blown and he needed our help?

There'd been a time when I barely commanded enough power to kindle a magelight. Those days were gone. Thanks to Cailleach, and more lately Arianrhod, the nascent power within me was awake and kicking. A few years back I might have wanted to go after Blake, but I'd have known I'd just be in the way. Now I could genuinely provide something useful.

I started for the cave entrance but pulled myself up short, relief spilling through me. Because my magical senses were deployed, I sensed Blake returning about the same time the dirt under my feet heaved and groaned. Great. We did not need an earthquake to complicate things.

Hedrek squawked. I felt rather than saw him summon power in case we had to leave fast. Rocks clattered against one another, falling from where they'd been stuck in the walls and ceiling. I sidestepped to avoid being flattened by a boulder the size of a compact car.

Blake burst through the entry, his expression like a thundercloud with brows drawn together and his forehead a mass of wrinkles.

"Damn it." He punched the air with a fist. Power flowed from him, encompassing Hedrek and me.

"Damn it, what? Is Roya okay?" I shouted to be heard over the increasing boom of falling rocks and roiling dirt.

"Roya's fine. Or she was when I left her. It's Earth. She's tired of the Cait sullying her realm. She asked me to get rid of them." Breath huffed from Blake. "Guess she didn't like my answer."

"Which was?" I pressed.

"That I was working on it," Blake replied.

"Nay. She wanted instant results," Hedrek hooted.

"Naught is instant with the Cait," Blake sputtered.

"Their response to this will be." I jumped again to escape being hit. A lion-sized chunk of rock crashed within a couple of inches of where I'd been standing.

Booming from below joined noise from above. If all the Orcs in Tolkien's fantasies had risen as an army with wolves baying, it wouldn't have been much noisier.

I grabbed Blake's arm. "We have to get out of here."

Talk about stating the obvious. As it was, we might have to teleport since I doubted a clear path remained through the warren of tunnels.

"Agreed. I'll round up Roya and the cats," Blake said.

"Not alone, you won't."

Dust filled my nose and mouth; breathing became more of a struggle. Why was the Earth goddess so all-fired anxious to rid herself of the Cait now? She'd had many opportunities before.

"See you outside." The murky air around the owl took on an incandescent glow. When it cleared, he was gone.

"We'll try the passageway," Blake said and grabbed my arm. We raced down its length. Something bright flashed nearly blinding me. "Sorry," Blake said, not breaking his pace. "Had to take my barrier down."

Squalling, hissing, yowling rose above the din of falling rocks. Clearly, the meeting had broken up, and the Cait who hadn't teleported out of here were trying to escape the old-fashioned way: on foot.

It complicated matters. Surely, they hadn't left Roya and the cats in the meeting hall. They could be anywhere.

Blake ground to a halt a few meters before where our side tunnel joined the main passageway. Usually, when he casts enchantments, it's a quiet proposition. This time, power arced between his hands. I assumed he was pulling out all the stops to locate his changeling Sidhe. I was worried about Roya, but not as concerned as he was. She'd survived clan wars and being subsumed by a Cait. That woman had resources. And she could teleport. The ones I was worried about were Abel and Marika. Not that garden variety alley cats weren't scrappy, resourceful fighters, but they'd have a hell of a hard time digging their way to the surface if the primary entrance fell in. Or was blocked.

I rocked from foot to foot to keep from falling to my knees.

The feel of Blake's power wrapped around me as he resurrected his warding. He beckoned to me, and we surged into a mass of Cait all heading in the opposite direction. It was worse than being a sole salmon fighting her way upstream. No way to avoid Cait running into us, but hysteria kept them from recognizing they hadn't careened off one another.

"Where'd they leave Roya?" I asked not bothering with telepathy. The noise level was such no one could hear me.

"Dungeon, or what passes for one." He spat the words. "She's beneath this level by many meters.

So much for potential allies. The minute events went south, the Cait couldn't wait to jettison Roya and presumably the cats.

"Are Abel and Marika with her?"

"Not sure. My links with them are erratic. They're still alive, but it's all I know."

He took a hard right down another side corridor. Damn. There must have been a hundred of them. This one branched, leading us ever lower. "The Cait couldn't have built all this," I mumbled.

"They didn't."

The temperature was definitely dropping; my breath made white puffs in front of me. I expected more by way of explanation, but it didn't come. After a couple more hairpin twists and turns, I asked, "Who did?"

"Satan and his underlings. We entered his territory a while back."

Mmph. Good to know.

My nostrils twitched seeking proof. Mostly, I still smelled the Cait, but every once in a while, I caught a whiff of sulfur with threads of ozone. Fear marched up my body, twisting my stomach into a knot. I've had run ins with shadow wraiths before. They're Satan's minions albeit a fairly minor subset. Minor though they were, they were pretty bad. I'd come perilously close to being captured.

That time, they'd come to me. I've rarely entered the nether realm willingly.

Pull it together, an inner voice ordered.

Solid advice. Because I wasn't paying close attention, I pitched up against Blake's back.

"Ooph. Why are we..." My words ran down when I saw iron grating set into a low, rounded gateway. Apparently, the king of Hell wasn't taking any chances on his minions escaping. Most magic wielders are sensitive to iron. I'm not one of them.

Blake grunted as his skin came into contact with rusty bars. I heard the sizzle as flesh burned. Hip butting him, I pushed him aside. "Let me."

The metal didn't singe me, but neither was I able to get it to budge. No latch; nothing readily visible, anyway.

Letting go, I eyed the barrier. Next to me, Blake's power soared as he jumped us to the far side.

"This is bullshit," he growled and pelted down a steep set of risers.

I had questions. Like how much farther to Roya, but I'd find out soon enough. We'd left the boom and rumble of falling earth behind long since. I'd actually trade an earthquake for Hell any day, but no one offered me that choice. The earlier chill gave way to heat so pervasive sweat trickled down my back and sides. I brushed it off my forehead before it could drip into my eyes and sting.

Where before the walls had been damp, now they were so dry the air filled with dust. Blake stopped abruptly and stared at an expanse of crumbling clay. Something that looked like a laser flared from his extended fingertips. It carved a trail in the wall until he made a 90 degree turn. With a groan, the wall settled, obliterating his cut.

He angled his head and flared his wings to the sides. Tendrils of blue-and-violet caressed the wall, examining it for weak spots. At least I assumed that was what he sought.

"Wait here," he announced at length.

I pushed a wing aside and hooked an arm through his. "Nope."

He looked sidelong at me. "Roya should be on the far side of this wall, but I don't have a clear picture of how it's laid out. I might teleport into something solid." He arched a brow. "Have you ever done that?"

I shook my head.

"Didn't think so. It's quite unpleasant."

Focusing a thread of seeking magic, I probed the wall.

Roya's changeling energy pinged back clean and clear. I dug deeper, intent on seeing if Abel and Marika were with her. They could have been, but something blocked my investigation.

Curious if Blake and I were working off the same picture, I asked, "You only get so far and then everything turns black?"

He rocked back on his heels and folded his wings across his back. "Aye. Not black so much as I can't see any further." Breath whooshed from him. "I can't carve an opening to crawl through. If I do, the whole shebang will fall on our heads."

"Maybe not. Looked as if the wall is self-healing." I paused. "What concerns me is tripping an alarm. If I were them, I'd have set one to ensure Roya didn't escape."

Blake snapped his fingers. "Of course. You're a genius, Abria."

I offered a broad smile. "Glad you appreciate me, but what precisely did I come up with that's brilliant."

"The reason you run into blackness, and I can't see clearly, is because they warded Roya's cell so she can't teleport out of there."

"What now?" I placed the flats of my palms on the wall, intent on a deeper look, and jumped back fast. "Ouch!" When I turned my hands over, they were red.

"Which is why I used magic rather than anything more direct."

I bristled. "Look. I brushed against the walls on our way here, and nothing happened."

"They didn't have anything to hide back there. Wait here. This is a job for one."

Before I could argue, he broke into motes of light.

"Oh no, you don't," I muttered and summoned power of my own, intent on following him through. My magic was listless, slow to respond. Did the million tons of earth on top of me have a dampening effect? Funny. I hadn't noticed it before, but then I hadn't tried to do much with my ability since leaving the cavern with the pool.

As I cobbled power this way and that trying to hit critical velocity for a teleport spell, I reached for Hedrek. *"Where are you?"*

"Outside. Cait are everywhere. The whole cave system collapsed."

I fist pumped the air, hoping some of the Cait would be buried for good.

"Are Marika and Abel with them?"

"No...Wait a minute. Yes, I just caught a glimpse. It was tough to tell since a lot of the Cait are in their cat form."

"'Are they all right?"

"Seem to be."

Whew. One less thing to worry about. I considered telling Blake, but Roya would take care of that.

"Can you gather them and teleport out of there?" I sucked in a breath waiting for his answer. It would be simpler to only have to worry about Blake and Roya.

"Maybe. If I do, I have to get it right the first time. Are you sure you don't want to leave them in place? The Cait appear to have accepted them, which gives us the spies we hoped for."

I closed my teeth over my lower lip, thinking. While I

hated the thought of leaving any ally in the hands of the Cait, still we'd have a way of learning their next steps. They no longer had a headquarters. Would they build another? Go off-world? Move up the timeline to attack the other Sidhe in an attempt to take Underhill for themselves?

My control-freak genes were in full rebellion when I replied, *"Leaving it up to you. If they appear in distress, please try to extricate them. So long as they're doing okay, it's smarter to leave them in place. Once we have Roya, we can set up shop somewhere close."*

The owl didn't answer, but there wasn't really anything more to say.

I assessed the rickety stack of power floating in front of me. It might be enough to move me through the wall. Blake should have been back by now. If he'd jumped into Roya's cell, snagging her and returning should have been a five-minute proposition.

Emphasis on the *should* part since he'd been gone for at least half an hour.

"Blake?"

No reply.

I tugged my working closer to my body. Should I loose my spell? What if I repeated whatever Blake had done and ended up just as trapped? I wanted to help, not hinder. Meant I had to be smart about this. Perhaps a different angle would yield something I hadn't yet added into the equation.

I trotted smartly deeper into the belly of Hell. The path was relatively flat in this section, and it curved to the right. I touched the wall again; this time it didn't burn me. Excitement surged. If the walls weren't reactive here, maybe I'd be able to sneak through them unnoticed, rescue Blake and Roya, and teleport us all the fuck out of here.

I'm not exactly claustrophobic...so long as I don't focus on the many tons of dirt and rock above my head. Some people fear drowning. For me, suffocation gets me going every time it rears its head. I've had nightmares about digging my way out from under cave-ins.

Don't think about that. Not now. Strong advice. For once, I listened to myself.

With zero warning. No noise. No fanfare. Nothing. The dusty clay beneath my feet opened. I clawed at the rim of the ever-widening hole. It crumbled beneath my touch, and I plummeted into fetid blackness.

Before my power scattered hither, thither, and yon, I gathered it close and held it in abeyance. Fear caught up, coating my tongue with a metallic tang. I'd been tumbling; I twisted so I was upright and curled into a ball with my arms around my knees.

I couldn't see. Switching to my third eye didn't help. High-pitched buzzing battered my ears. It grew louder as I fell. Every instinct screamed for me to launch a teleport spell and make a run for it, but I wasn't at all certain I had enough juice to pull it off. Wasting power would make my situation worse.

From far above, I heard Blake calling my name. Crap. I'd been beyond stupid to move from where he'd left me.

"Blake." I paid out the tiny bit of magic needed for telepathy.

"I have Roya. Where are you?"

It was tough to answer. I have a lot of pride. My first

bent was to tell him to leave, that I'd figure this out on my own. Except he wouldn't. Leave me, that is. I knew him better than that. He was like the Sidhe version of a goddamned Marine.

They never left men behind. Neither did he.

"Fell through a hole," I blurted. *"Twenty meters down the corridor."*

Someone else must have been listening because rocks, grit, and dirt cascaded through the opening I could barely see above me. Twist and turn as I might, I couldn't avoid everything. After a fist-sized rock clonked the top of my head, I fashioned some of my precious power into a ward and wrapped myself inside.

Blake would have a harder time finding me, but at least there'd be some of me left to find. Suddenly, I was falling faster. Whoever was orchestrating this was getting bored—or running out of magic. The latter would be very good news since mine was mostly fresh at this point.

Expending as little enchantment as possible, I crafted a cushion of air beneath me. Turned out to be fortuitous since I hit bottom with a *thud* that could have been so much worse.

I got my feet under me and scrambled upright. I still couldn't see shit, so I summoned the palest of mage lights.

And wished I hadn't.

Half a dozen demons circled me, moving nearer with the speed of light. I'd never actually seen one before, but I'd have recognized them anywhere with their seven-foot height, scaled hides, horns, cloven hoofs, and beady red eyes. Obscene phalluses hung almost to the ground. Some did. Others were erect and curving against belly scales.

They spoke a language I'd never heard before. Guttural with a predominance of consonants, it chilled me even absent content. Fear raced along every nerve ending threatening to swamp me, but I've never been a coward.

Reshaping my existing ward, I formed it into what I hoped would hold them off for a while. If it worked as intended, they could see me and hear me, but not reach through the barrier.

I stood tall and turned in a circle staring at each monster in turn. "Nice of you to invite me to the party, boys, but you can all go fuck yourselves."

Ha! They might speak a different language, but they sure as hell understood English. Roaring like madmen—who knew? Maybe they were—they threw themselves against my warding.

It strained, but held.

A rattled sigh shook me. So far, so good. Would my fortune last until Blake located me? Surely, he wouldn't be foolish enough to take on a demon horde, but he could leverage power to jump us out of here.

I hoped.

"Keep the faith, sweetie," I whispered. "This could turn out better than I think it will."

Or not.

One of the demons had grabbed my barrier and was working on shredding it with his teeth. Sparks flew. The spot he gnawed developed a hole. I patched it, but another grew by its side. Shouting encouragement—or something—

his twisted kin each picked a prime location. Soon the noise from grinding teeth was all I could hear.

This was my own goddamned fault. I counted holes. Twenty or so would spell the end of my ward. I could pour more power into holding onto it as long as possible, or I could move on to Plan B. If I transitioned the magic in my ward to fight mode, maybe I could injure enough of them to buy me breathing space.

Dream on, sweetie.

Oh shut up. If you don't like my idea, I told my inner critic, *come up with something better.*

BLAKE

I bolted down the corridor, Roya by my side, and screeched to a halt when I saw the hole Abria had fallen through. Bits of rock and dirt were still tumbling through the opening as if it possessed a magnetic pull. Had she stumbled across a weak spot? Was this pure bad luck?

Roya crouched near the edge, but not so close as to risk being swept away. Guess she'd had more than her share of adventures for one day. Power flowed from her raised wrist stumps in shades of deep blue and shimmery gray. She turned and looked up at me.

"Someone knew Abria would be here," she muttered.

"How? I had no idea we'd take this route until I started following your energy."

Roya shrugged. "Who can tell about these things, but look at these." Where she pointed, runes morphed in and out of view. Sure enough, they carried a description of Abria.

And her name.

I ground my teeth until my jaws ached. Names held tremendous power. It would give demonspawn the upper hand once they got down and dirty with interrogations.

"Never going to happen," I growled.

"What isn't going to happen?" Roya sounded confused.

"No one is going to torture Abria."

"Not if we hurry. How can we get to her?" the changeling asked.

I felt grateful she hadn't pointed out torture was the least of what Abria was likely to face. There'd been a bounty on her head for centuries, but her enemies had only gotten serious about collecting on it recently.

Why now? What had changed?

Questions bumped heads with strategy until my mind turned into a rancid soup of discarded possibilities. "We need reinforcements," I mumbled.

"True, but if we wait for them to show up, we could lose her." Roya sprang to her feet and stood by my side.

Guilt cut deep. Roya had said "we." Of course, she had. But the only reason she was here was her misplaced loyalty to me, the mage who'd ripped her from her human family.

"Leave. Simpler for me to manage this on my own." My voice was purposefully gruff because I didn't want her to argue.

Roya repositioned herself until she faced me, leaving her back to the ever-widening hole. "Really?" She furled both russet brows. "Because if memory serves me it took both of us to extricate her from the between worlds place the Cait chucked her."

I softened my tone, placed a hand on her shoulder. "You saved her. I merely finished the job."

"See? I rest my case. It required us both." Her nostrils flared. "I don't care what happened in the far reaches of the past. I'm here. Use me to finish this."

"I ordered you to leave."

A small shrug. "And I refused. Next?"

One side of my mouth twitched into the start of a smile. Had I ever had control over any of the Sidhe? I suspected not. Someone had to lead the council, and so long as I wasn't overly heavy-handed, everyone offered support.

On paper.

When the rubber met the road, mages generally did as they chose. It was why the Cait had formed their own faction and left.

"Elwyn. We needed to get going. Ten minutes ago."

The use of my true name shocked me into action. The best way to find Abria was to shadow her trail. "They'll be expecting us," I said and draped warding over Roya and myself.

"Bring it on. I hate those bastards."

The venom in her voice surprised me. I've always viewed Roya as the changeling I left to guard one of many portals to Underhill and other worlds. My earlier guilt swelled and took wings. If I'd had the foresight to check on her, the problem with the Cait might not have burgeoned into where it stood today.

With one arm firmly around her, I jumped into the hole, guiding our way with the least amount of power possible.

The demons who'd captured Abria had surely alerted Satan by now. Or one of his princes.

They weren't stupid. They'd be expecting someone to show up, which meant they'd be ready. My task was to ensure I didn't waltz us into a trap. My night vision is exceptional, but there was no light in this place to amplify. Abria's scent and vestiges of her energy reassured me she'd fallen past our current point.

How far away was the bottom? Was there even one, or did this channel lead right into the fiery pit beneath Satan's realm? The question had a sobering effect. Risking a slender beam of light was preferable to falling into molten rock. The air currents shifted, carrying the reek of decaying flesh.

Rotten meat suggested putrescent corpses. Nasty as they were, they beat hellfire by a good big bunch. Instead of light, I opted for a thick layer of air beneath us to cushion our fall. A solid *thunk* said we'd reached bottom. Maybe not absolute bottom, but bottom for now.

My link with Abria lit like a beacon. She'd been in this very spot, and not all that long ago. No one was near; I'd have sensed them even if they were warded.

"This way." Roya tugged on my arm.

"Hold up. Let me check." The demons could have planted a scent track to send us chasing our tails. No help for it. I kindled a weak beam of light. We stood in the center of a small chamber perhaps ten meters across. Piles of bones littered the space. Some were human, a grisly reminder demons preferred to dine on mortals above all else. Rumors had circulated for millennia that only a small percentage of Hell-bound souls actually made it to the netherworld. The

rest turned into dinner for Satan's perpetually underfed horde.

They were dead anyway, but it still disgusted me. Even mortals who'd been wicked enough to end up here didn't deserve to end up on some fucker's menu. Ever methodical, I checked each of the entrances radiating outward from the cavern like spokes on a wagon wheel.

The difference between them was subtle. Lacking the link I had to Abria, I might not have keyed into the proper channel. I turned Roya toward a different corridor than she'd selected. *"This one. Stay close, within my ward, no matter what."*

She didn't respond. Not with words, but she fell in behind me, and we navigated twists and turns by feel, tripping over ever-present bones. My light was a dead giveaway no matter how much I dimmed its glow. After half a kilometer, we didn't need it. A faint, red glow illuminated the walls.

The stench thickened. Decay raised to a factor of ten. Maybe nothing finished rotting down here and just stank in perpetuity. I could see demons living in squalor, but Satan is quite fastidious. I've met him a time or two—when he wanted something—and he was always impeccably turned out. His princes follow suit. Most of them, anyway. Belphegor, prince of sloth, being a notable exception.

The guttural sounds of demonspeak wafted our way. I slowed to listen. Perhaps I'd hear something that would assist with Abria's rescue. According to energy pounding along the link I'd established between us, she was close.

Why in the goddess's name hadn't she stayed where I'd left her?

Be fair, an inner voice suggested in silken tones. *You didn't exactly forbid her to move.*

Even if I had, she would have ignored me.

Enough of this. I angled my head, listening intently. The speaker was rambling on about taking full credit for Abria's capture. Would the others let him get away with that? I didn't have to wait long for my answer.

Before, the voices had been a muted buzz. They swelled in intensity as everyone else mobbed the speaker, presumably pounding him into oblivion. From the sound of things, there were way more demons than I'd counted on.

I focused my mind voice for Roya only. *"Stealth is the only way we'll manage this. Stick close."*

"You're going to remain invisible?"

"Aye, unless you have a better idea."

She shook her head. I gave her points for guts. I'd ordered her away, and she'd ignored me. Instructing her to wait in this corridor would meet with similar results.

My plan, what there was of it, was simple. Get in, take advantage of the brawl still in progress to snag Abria, and teleport the fuck out of Hell. The only unknown was if the latter was possible. I'd never tried it. Some locations don't lend themselves to magical journeys.

Guess I was about to find out.

Done waiting, I surged forward with Roya shadowing me. The corridor flared into a high, rounded entry a hundred paces from where we'd stood as I eavesdropped. The thump of fists barreling into scales was punctuated with curses, squeals, and shrieks. The copper stench of blood mingled with all the other rotten smells bombarding my nostrils.

I edged to the side and took stock. At least fifty demons were piling atop one another. No one was sitting this one out. Anger flowed so hot, it made reddish waves in the fetid air. The Sidhe have tempers, but in all my long years ruling my wayward flock, I've never seen us plow into one another with anywhere near this level of gusto.

I might have misinterpreted, but the demons seemed to be having a grand old time. I scanned the cavern. It was large. Maybe fifty meters across. Where was Abria? Every sense I had corroborated she was here, but I couldn't see her.

Roya sidled next to me and pointed upward.

A filthy cage made of rusty metal was suspended high in the air. Try as I might, I couldn't determine what it attached to. The metal made it impossible for me to snatch Abria from her aerial post. Nay. I needed the cage on the ground and a wrecking bar to pry the latch.

I had time. The brawl was still escalating. It wouldn't be over any time soon. Whoever had masterminded the location of Abria's confinement had been brilliant. They must have known metal would stymie most magic-wielders, so they could go about the business of dividing up the bounty spoils undisturbed.

I'm capable of many things including flight, but I can't fly warded. The magics are incompatible.

And then, I remembered Hedrek.

Conceivably, a blow from his mighty beak could spring the cage door. I raised my mind voice and called his name.

He didn't respond. *Mmph.* Answered one question. Hell, at least at this deep a level, muffled my power beyond its boundaries. Meant teleporting wouldn't work, either.

Abria lay so still I feared the worst. *"Abria. Darling."*

"Go away. I'm figuring this out."

Annoyance flared. Same cheeky bitch who'd told me to hit the bricks more times than I could count. I didn't dignify her comment with a reply, but her courage in the face of tough odds was one of the reasons I was so smitten.

"I'm serious, Blake. I got myself into this mess, and—"

"Shut up."

A murder of crows, black wings gleaming in the low light, swept into the cave. High-pitched squalling drew my attention downward. Hundreds of huge gray rats poured out of all four entry points to the cavern.

A reluctant smile parted my lips. Of course. She'd put out the call to her original allies. And they'd dropped everything to come to her aid. Rats crawled onto every pile of demons, biting and ripping as they went. Crows circled Abria's prison cawing raucously.

"Quiet," I urged. Not unlike my subjects, they ignored me.

One of the demons, a black-scaled fellow with a barrel chest, long, curving horns, and three blood-red eyes fought his way out from under two of his brethren. Pointing skyward, he shrieked, "She's getting away," in demonspeak.

The brawl ended as quickly as it had begun. Every demon in the place ran toward where the cage hung suspended. The rats changed up their attack, grabbing onto tails and rumps and obscenely long scrotal sacks. Demons batted at them, but the rats clung tenaciously.

Crows still circled the cage so thickly I couldn't see through their feathered forms. Suddenly, as if controlled by a single mind, they wheeled and flew from the cave. The cage was empty. Abria had gone.

I reached for her through my link but couldn't find her.

A barrage of angry demonspeak, and then the fight started up all over again, this time with even more grit. They'd had quite the prize.

And lost it.

Not that I made a habit of underestimating Abria, but I'd never make that mistake again. I hadn't thought I could teleport out of here, but she'd managed it handily.

The birds were gone. The rats squealed happily. I figured they'd leave when they were good and ready. Demon flesh might smell like crap to me, but maybe it hit the delicacy list in rat-dom.

With all the ruckus, no one had noticed us. I wanted to keep it that way, so I backed us up the way we'd come. Partway down the corridor, I turned and fell into a lope. No one followed us, but I hadn't expected them to.

"See. She didn't need us after all." Roya sounded as proud as if she'd been the one to engineer Abria's escape.

"She might have." Defensiveness crept under the corners of my words.

Roya ran next to me. She elbowed me in the ribs. "Not the Middle Ages any longer."

"I kind of miss damsels in distress," I joked.

"Then you should have picked someone else for your mate."

Bitterness lined her words. I didn't blame her. If she'd lived in a different time, her father wouldn't have seen it as his right to lop off her hands.

"Thanks for coming with me." I tried a different tack to refocus the conversation.

"I'm Sidhe. We do what's necessary for our own."

"Doesn't mean I can't thank you."

"Nay, but it means you don't have to."

We'd reached a point where I hoped I could jump us out of here. I'd had more than enough of the Cait and Hell for one day. Careful to keep my warding in place, I launched a travel spell. Lethargic at first, it finally took off.

The reek and desperation of Satan's realm dissipated, leaving us suspended in darkness. The first clean breath in hours filled my lungs. I sucked air like a dying man and blessed every deity who'd ever walked I didn't have to remain in Hell—or with my Cait cousins—another moment.

There'd be a rematch soon, but not today.

"Where did Abria go?" Roya asked.

"Good question, but she had enough magic—and wits —to finesse her own escape. I have faith she made it to safety."

Roya's gaunt features spread into a rare smile. "It's about time. I told you she didn't need rescuing."

I wrapped an arm around the changeling whose loyalty I didn't deserve and replied, "You did, indeed."

CHAPTER 17
ABRIA

When I was done cursing myself twenty times over for falling into a trap with my name smeared all over it, I moved on to more productive pursuits. Like getting the fuck out of Hell. The kicker was when half a dozen beefy demons chucked me in a cage and suspended it from goddess-only-knew what.

At least they left me alone after that. Mostly because they got into some sort of argument that rapidly moved from words to blows. Damn, but I wished I knew their language. The brawl gave me thinking time. When two of them had grabbed me the second I hit bottom, I'd fought back. Comported myself fairly well, but my Plan B had been an abysmal failure. I took out a single demon before the rest of the pack piled on top of me smothering me with their stench and sheer bulk.

Ick.

Brute force wasn't going to get me out of here.

After that, I pretty much played dead. It was when they tossed me in the metal cage, no doubt assuming iron is as deadly to me as it is to most mages. Stupid of them.

I swore I wouldn't sacrifice animal lives for my own, wouldn't leverage their loyalty if it put them in harm's way. In this case, they came to me unbidden. I'd never guessed any of my cohort lived in this place. Maybe they didn't. It wasn't the time nor the place for detailed conversation—or to order them to leave. They wouldn't have no matter what I said.

Rats dove into the melee, dishing out additional punishment as they tore chunks of demon flesh from twitching bodies. Crows circled my aerial perch, effectively shielding me from sight.

It was exactly the opportunity I needed.

And then Blake showed up. Damn him. I told him to leave before anyone noticed him. Or maybe I just told him to leave. Regardless, he ignored me. Fine. Two could play that game. Best thing I could do was vanish. Once he saw I wasn't here, he'd leave too.

Hopefully before the demons noticed him. And Roya.

Her loyalty touched me. I'd saved her once from a Cait. She was here to return the favor. Blake would never have ordered her into danger. He still felt guilty for turning her from human to changeling.

At least she was all right. I hoped Abel and Marika were too. They weren't with Roya. Did it mean they were still with the Cait, masquerading as allies?

I swiped a mental hand across my mind. Time for all my questions, but later.

With as much subtlety as I could muster, I wove earth and fire into a journey spell, adding a touch of air to kindle the mix. The cage fell away instantly. I barely had time to draw warding around myself before thick jungle surrounding the entrance to the Cait's borrowed realm bloomed around me.

Cait Sidhe ran every which way, squalling like spoiled children. They have many things in common with their feline counterparts, including a serious entitlement mentality. Still aiming for understated, I hunted for Abel and Marika.

Breath whooshed from me when I located them. Safe. My friends were safe. The cats stood in a growing group of Cait Sidhe. No one seemed to be paying them much heed. Interesting they hadn't trusted Roya despite her credible cover story, but the cats fit right in.

I hated to leave them here, but it might be the right thing to do until we had a sense which way the Cait winds were blowing. Unwilling to make the decision for them, I activated the enchantment linking me to anything with fur, feathers, or scales. To be on the safe side, I kept my communication brief.

"Stay or go?" They'd know it was me. No need for more words.

Abel rubbed his head against Marika's. Good move since his mind speech would be more noticeable than mine. *"Mmrroowwwstay."*

"Okay. I'll remain close."

With one thing decided, I hunted for Hedrek. The owl

was enormous—and obvious. Since I couldn't see him anywhere, he was either warded or he'd left.

A pair of Cait barreled into me. Striking like all Sidhe, the pair had long silver hair and amber eyes. They looked so much alike, they had to be related. Arched cheekbones, pointed chins, and stubby dark wings completed the picture. The wings in question twitched with irritation.

Oh-oh. They may be spoiled, but they're far from brain-damaged.

One drew back, hissing. "Show yourself."

Yeah. Right.

He dragged a rapier from a jeweled scabbard. Hanging around while he jabbed the air held zero appeal. I hustled off, angling for a thick place in the foliage where no one else would stumble over me.

"Who was that?" one of the Cait snarled.

"How should I know?" his buddy countered as he jabbed and sliced the place I'd stood.

"Not demons," Cait number one said. "They're too arrogant to conceal themselves."

I bit my lower lip to muffle laughter. Talk about pots calling kettles black.

Still arguing about the enigma of who they'd plowed into, they joined a nearby group of Cait. I returned to searching for Hedrek.

Blake and Roya should be here soon. Unless something unspeakable had happened in Hell. Weariness washed over me in waves. If they didn't show soon, I'd go back and investigate. The absolute last thing I wanted was to return to the stinking, fetid squalor that was Hell, but Blake hadn't hesitated when he thought I was in danger.

If it came down to it, neither would I.

A soft hooting in my mind told me the owl had found me. I like problems that solve themselves. His appearance saved me the trouble of locating him. *"Where are you?"* I asked.

"A hundred meters to the south."

I initiated a quick jump and joined him. We were far enough away from the displaced Cait, I jettisoned my ward. It's a real power hog, and my resources were dwindling.

"You look bad. What happened?" Hedrek perched on a low branch of a gum tree.

"You don't want to know."

"Aye, I do. You stink of demon."

Busted. I sketched out most of what had transpired. "Anyway," I went on, "once I freed myself—with help from some rats and crows—I asked Abel and Marika what they wanted to do."

"They're staying," the owl informed me.

I nodded. Guess my conversation with them wasn't the first on that particular topic. "So long as they're staying, we need to stick close." Responsibility weighed heavy. I'd be damned if something happened to the cats who'd volunteered at my behest.

But I was focusing on them to avoid thinking about Blake and Roya. The window within which I'd allotted them to show up was rapidly shrinking.

"Can you keep an eye on the cats?" I asked.

"Why? Where are you going?"

"Blake and Roya should be back by now. I'm going after them."

Hedrek clacked his beak a couple of times. "Bad idea."

"No it's not." I took a few paces back and looked up at the owl. "They risked themselves going after me."

"Blake is resourceful. He'll figure something out."

"What if he doesn't?"

Hedrek fluttered to the ground. "You should search for the ley lines. Between the confusion here, and what you described in Hell, there'll not be a better time."

"Where do I even begin?" This was Hedrek; no need to pretend I knew more than I did. "Arianrhod only mentioned them in passing. Her opinion was my power wasn't robust enough to take on the project."

"I disagree or I wouldn't have suggested you go. Finding them will be the hard part," the owl informed me. "Once you locate one, you simply follow it until you find the broken parts."

"Why are you so certain I can fix them?" I demanded.

"'Tis a task you were born to."

If it were true, why had I only just found out about it recently? I didn't give voice to that thought, but Hedrek is skilled at reading my mind.

"I still think I should go after Blake."

The owl fluttered close, rubbing his feathers against my leg. His head reached to waist level. "Trust me. I carry the goddess's blessing and will."

No need to ask which goddess. He was referring to Arianrhod. She was who'd scared him up for me, and I'd always suspected they had some type of bond.

He must have sensed my ambivalence because he said, "I'll look out for Abel and Marika."

"Blake and Roya?"

"Not worried about them."

Yeah, he'd already said as much.

Either I left. Or I didn't. Pretty simple when you cut meat from bone. I did trust the owl. He'd been nothing but kind to me. Before I could think it to death—something that always leads to inertia on my part—I pulled power close, visualized a spot deep below the earth's surface, and departed.

Ley lines carry magical energy, but it was precious little to go on. I assumed they ran near Earth's molten core, but they could just as easily connect worlds. Would I be better off starting on a border world?

If so, which one? There were hundreds, and I'd only visited a scant handful.

The crystal-lined cave I'd aimed for flared to life around me. I kindled a mage light, enjoying the bounce and glitter as it reflected off faceted surfaces. Once, this had been a special place for me. It was where I'd hidden when I'd first run away from the Celts. Something about its energy—or frequency—had hidden me so well no one had come close to finding me.

Or so I'd thought at the time. Closer to the truth, no one had bothered to look.

I paced in a tight circle. Where to go from here?

An hour later I wasn't any closer to an answer. I could strike out blind and spend the next hundred years search- ing. Not a pleasant proposition, particularly not when Hedrek had intimated now was the time to strike. If I tarried, the lines could be guarded by my enemies. Those who'd rather take me down than allow me an opportunity to correct whatever faux pas my making had created.

My heart was beating too fast. I took several full, deep breaths to calm myself. If ever I needed a cool head, it was now.

The beginnings of an answer took shape. Reluctantly, I opened my magical senses seeking the source of my ability. This was new for me. I've always shrouded as much of my skill as possible. Up until rather recently, I hadn't believed I had any magic at all to speak of.

Nothing beyond my affinity for animals.

Laying my magic bare was akin to peeling an onion. I thought I was done, but another layer cropped up. I was vulnerable throughout the process, so naked it terrified me. Never mind, no one had ever found this hiding place before.

There was always a first time.

My earth eyes were closed. Information flowed through my third eye and my other psychic senses. For the longest time, they bounced from this to that to the other, but suddenly something deep inside me shifted.

A path formed, and I knew exactly where I needed to go.

Blood dripped into my mouth; I stopped biting my lower lip. This would be far more difficult than I expected. So challenging, I might not be able to pull it off alone.

"Except I have no choice," I mumbled.

In addition to the path, for the first time I caught a glimpse of the future. Of me treading that path.

By myself.

I've never had seer ability, yet I didn't doubt the truth

spread before me. Fate catches us up when we least expect it. I had to return to Hell. The last place I wanted to go. The ley lines spanned worlds, but they ran through the bowels of Hell, and it was the only place I'd be able to access them. On other worlds, they were guarded by monsters far worse than demonkind.

I don't know that. Not for sure.

Nice try. I answered myself.

I needed rest, food, lots of things.

"Another nice try. Get moving, sister. It won't get easier with waiting." This time, I spoke aloud to steady myself.

I took stock of my magical reservoir. If everything went perfectly, I might have enough power left to repair the ley lines and exit Hell. It would be close, far closer than I liked.

No help for it.

With a last look around at the cave that had been both refuge and comfort, I aimed for the river Styx. Charon had befriended me once. Maybe I could count on him to shield me, hide my essence, and pretend I was just one more newly dead soul bound for Hell.

Good plan if it worked. If not, he'd summon Satan, and I'd be lost in a mad scramble to escape. Not only that, but I'd also have killed the element of surprise and shut off any possibility of approaching the ley lines in his realm.

A deep sigh burst from me. I cut it off at its roots.

Today was all about trust and instincts and going for it in the face of incomplete information. Pretty much the story of my life ever since that blasted battle in the Rait Castle courtyard.

The spell I needed was already there. More proof, as if I

needed any, I was no longer mistress of anything but following a course laid out for me long ago.

"Next stop, the river Styx," I murmured as the cave fell away. Dousing my mage light, I waited out the transit in darkness.

Had I made the right choice? I'd find out in good time.

CHAPTER 18

ABRIA

Not too long after I'd made good on my escape from the Celts—and before I found the crystal cave—I'd stumbled across a passageway carved deep beneath Mount Olympus. Trying to put as much distance as I could between myself and the spot the Celts had imprisoned me, I kept to the shadows.

The passageway was promising. Wide and winding, it might provide just the escape hatch I needed. In those days, I wasn't picky. And I was running scared. I had no idea I could teleport, so any traveling was done via my two feet. I sprinted for a long while, so long my muscles turned to lead.

Finally, too weary to continue, I curled into a declination in the dirt wall and fell asleep. A warm, wet something on my face jolted me to consciousness. My eyes snapped open. I tried to squirm away, but it was hopeless. No matter which way I turned, the same heat tracked down my face, my head, my body.

Between sleep-fuzz and terror, it took far longer than it should have for me to recognize a dog's tongue. Except it was three of them because this dog had three heads. It was how I met Cerebrus. A larger-than-life hound, he blocked my efforts to run with his gray-furred body.

If he'd wanted to injure me, he'd have used far more than his tongue. I'd just reached out a tentative hand to stroke his rough fur when a deep, booming voice called, "What have we here?"

Charon had found me, but I had no idea who he was. Garbed in homespun gray robes the same color as his hound, he had a white beard that reached the ground, empty eye sockets, and gnarled fingers with many silver rings.

I gasped out something about being sorry for trespassing and that I'd be on my way, but Charon wasn't having any of it. Clearly, he'd figured out I wasn't his usual customer. Perhaps he sensed the power in me, power I had no idea I possessed.

By then, I was babbling, but if they'd meant me harm, I'd have known. And if they were in cahoots with the Celts, it was news to me since I'd never seen either the old man or his dog.

Charon rubbed a bony finger across my damp cheeks. It was how I knew I was crying. Next, he scooped me into his arms and took off at a lope with Cerebrus next to us. I don't remember much after that, only bits and pieces. I'm sure he altered my memories to ensure I didn't retain enough to tell anyone about my encounter.

Perhaps he was forbidden to hobnob with the living.

Meals came and went. We may have talked, but I don't remember any of it. One day, I came back to myself on a grassy knoll in bright sunlight. I felt terribly exposed, but I was alone. I could have been with Charon for a day or a week or a year. At least, I knew his name. And the name of his dog. He'd told me my tongue would split in two if ever I mentioned either—or my time with them.

As if I had anyone to confide in. Until my not-so-chance encounter with Blake, I'd been the quintessential loner. Something about letting him into my life had kicked the door wide open for Birgit, Cailleach, and a host of others.

Time passed in my young life—a whole lot of it. Once I was certain the Celts weren't after me, I searched for entry points to Charon's realm, but I never did locate the underground passage where he'd found me. I wanted to thank him. So few people had been kind to me, it seemed proper to recognize those who were.

Long after I'd given up my search, he found me in the dark of a wintry night in northern Scotland. Cerebrus wasn't with him. We talked for hours, and this time he didn't blitz my mind. He did explain it wasn't wise to look for him, that the place I'd been wasn't a spot allowed to the living—except for him and his hound.

Memories are funny things. My brief history with the boatman flashed through my head as I urged my journey spell to drop me on the far side of the river Styx. Better that side so I wouldn't have to cross it. Unlike my early attempts to locate this spot, my magic had expanded by a factor of a hundred. If I couldn't break through into the boatman's realm now, it wasn't meant to be.

I had no doubt he'd remember me, but it didn't mean he'd support my quest or be pleased to see me when he'd forbidden me to hunt him down.

The feel of my magic changed. I had to be near my destination. I warded myself out of an abundance of caution in case Charon wasn't alone. Hell, he might not even be there. If he wasn't, I'd set out anyway. He'd sense an intruder in his realm soon enough and come after me.

The sound of rushing water filled my ears. Had the river gained momentum since my last visit? I clunked down harder than I liked, so hard breath whooshed from me, and my ribs ached. Luckily, I landed on mud rather than sharp rocks.

The river Styx held an odd phosphorescence that lit my surroundings. I was alone as I scrambled upright. And I'd come out on the far side of the river exactly as I'd planned. Myth and legends claim it serves as a dividing line between the realm of the living and the land of the dead.

Since I was firmly on the dead side, a place I didn't belong, I hustled forward. The sooner I found the lines, the sooner I could leave. I didn't expect I'd be fortunate enough to escape detection, but a woman can dream.

Fortune be damned. Disappointment thrummed through me. I'd hoped to renew my acquaintance with Charon and his hound.

Not why I'm here.

I ignored my inner nag.

This part of Hell wasn't nearly as obnoxious as the spot I'd been strung up in the cage. It smelled of water rather than rot. I shored up my warding and hustled. As I ran, I extended tendrils of magic to all sides. Why was this place so empty?

Souls arriving without the requisite coin were supposedly stuck on the other side of the Styx for a year and a day. But I hadn't sensed anyone over there, either.

Did I only think I was trotting through Hell's outer layers? Had someone played sorcerer, hijacked my spell, and sent me elsewhere?

The thought was disconcerting. And unlikely. Granted, I was beyond weary, but I'd have noticed the feel of alien magic. I ran past side passages branching this way and that.

Should I choose one of them?

What did these ley lines feel like?

Pfft. Was I woefully underprepared or what? If I could go back and rewrite history, I'd have made far better use of my time with Arianrhod. Mostly, we'd sparred with one another. Disappointment on her side, anger on mine. Regardless, I wished we'd been different with one another.

I couldn't hear the water any longer. My path branched and branched again. After the second choice point, I marked runes in the wall to guide my return journey. Assuming there was one, I might not have time to stop and ponder which way I'd come.

I'd try to teleport, but if I didn't have enough magic left, I'd be stuck leaving the same way I'd come.

Faint at first, demon reek grew thicker. Along with it, my throat tightened, and my stomach twisted sourly. How long since I'd eaten? Not that it mattered. No one could eat in the middle of this stench. Rot. Dead things. Decay.

Was I the only thing alive down here? Besides Hell's minions, that is.

I wasn't doing myself any favors with my mad dash deeper into Hell, so I ducked into a channel angling downward and steadied my breathing. It had degenerated into a ragged pant. Impossible to cover every angle, so I'd taken to sweeping my attention in a circle to check for enemies.

Effective, but exhausting.

"Think," I muttered.

If the lines were the source of my power, I should be able to home in on them by digging deep and following whatever popped up.

Can't be that simple.

Why not?

Ach, great. Now I was talking with myself. I squeezed my eyes shut. They felt hot, gritty, filled with bits of ground glass. I couldn't come up with a better idea, so I risked turning my attention inward to where my power dwells. Eyes shut, barely breathing, I sought the source of my ability.

Gray, voluminous clouds obscured my search; I pushed them aside, but they crowded back thicker than ever. Were the lines sentient? They almost had to be. Either that, or someone guarded their location.

The last option was unpleasant. Repairing whatever was wrong would take all my know-how. I didn't think I'd be able to do that and fight off some self-appointed guardian.

I pinched the bridge of my nose between two fingers. I was not thinking clearly. Or maybe not thinking at all. If anyone else had located the lines, they'd either have done the requisite repair—after all this was a mutual well, one we all drew from—or they'd have sabotaged the whole mess.

Cycling through various combinations of magic, I attacked the clouds that stood between me and determining how to proceed. No matter what I did, they refused to allow me to glean what I needed. I'd catch a glimpse, but never enough to proceed.

Crap.

I doubled up a fist and slammed it into the wall.

Pain shot up my arm, but a slice of clarity formed. Was misery the price of knowledge? Figuring it had to be a coincidence, I pounded the wall again. The opening in the clouds grew a few more centimeters.

Fine. I could do this. I'd been sacrificing myself for as long as I could remember.

Pound. Thud. Pound. Thud.

The salt smell of blood filled my nostrils.

Oh-oh. Not smart at all. Blood draws predators. I layered magic over my abraded knuckles. Had I gotten away with making a rookie mistake? I sucked in a tentative breath. Meanwhile, all the progress I'd made vanished. The shielding was thicker than before I'd begun.

"What are you doing here?"

Not his usual booming bass. Nothing warm nor welcoming at all, but I'd know Charon's voice anywhere. He'd seen right through my warding. Either my disguise wasn't nearly as bulletproof as I'd hoped, or his magic superseded mine by a good big bunch.

I voted for gate number two.

A hand closed around my shoulder. 'You shouldn't be here, lass. Penalties are steep."

I released my warding. Not much point hanging onto something that was useless and drained magic to boot. I squared my shoulders and looked at the boatman's empty eye sockets. He hadn't changed a bit in all the intervening years. To an outsider, he'd have appeared menacing, kind of like a personification of the grim reaper absent a sickle. But he'd been kind to me.

"I have no choice," I said.

"Explain yourself, but not here."

Before he leveraged power and whisked me elsewhere, I held up a hand. "It must be here. I am tasked with finding the ley lines, locating where my making broke them, and mending the damage."

"Why you?"

It was a fair question. "I've been hunted almost since the day the Celts made me. Something about my presence created a disturbance in the lines. Word got out, and I've been pursued ever since. Of late, the hunt has escalated until I have to watch my back every minute."

Charon drew his bushy grey brows together. "How will addressing the breach in the lines change that?"

"It might not, but I have to try."

Distant footsteps pounded toward us. "You've been discovered," Charon growled. "'Twas only a matter of time. Your essence disturbs the balance of Hell."

"Then let me go. I'm not leaving until I'm done."

"What if there is no 'done'? The lines do not show themselves willingly. Or at all, most of the time."

"I'm going anyway," I said, aiming for a steadfast tone and almost accomplishing it.

"No matter what the outcome, this task will change you." Charon paused before adding, "There will be no going back."

I started to ask change me how, except it didn't matter. Nothing that came out of his mouth would alter my chosen course. It couldn't. I had to do this or spend the rest of forever on the defensive.

"In the months and years to come, remember you asked for this." He placed an index finger beneath my chin, tipping it upward. A series of images filled my mind. Sort of like telepathy but with pictures rather than words.

"Got it," I breathed. "Thank---" Before I could finish, he was gone.

The footsteps were growing louder. Past time for me to get on with things. Charon had drawn me a map. All I had to do was follow it.

Focusing my enchantment, I aimed for a spot far below, a place encased by rock and fire. I didn't think the demons would follow me—if they even could. But I wasn't certain of anything.

Relieved to have a direction, and even more relieved Charon hadn't summarily booted me from his domain, I fought my way through an increasingly claustrophobic journey spell. I'd get close to my objective, but then I wasn't close at all. I cycled through air, earth, fire, and water. The later was worthless.

So was everything except fire. Surrounded by flames so hot they singed my clothing, my hair, even my eyes, I soldiered on. Power ran through me at an alarming rate. Would I have enough to even get to the proper spot, let alone do anything but sink into a worthless heap once I arrived?

Uh-uh, I chided. *Visualize results.*

It's the first rule of magic, and one I'd let slip to the sidelines. The moment I held my objective—an image Charon had shared—firmly in mind, I dropped onto the shore of a fiery lake. Heat blazed through a grotto with the lake in its center. Trying not to think about the bazillion tons of dirt and rocks over my head, I hunted for the source of the flames.

Defying all the laws of physics, the lake was on fire. Somehow, its waters fed the blaze and kept it going. Worse, an eerie phosphorescence bound the flames, leading them in a hypnotic dance. One that immobilized me if I stared too long.

Stretched next to the lake lay a glittery rope. As big around as my thigh, it pulsed with untold strength. It had to be the ley line extending as far as I could see in both directions.

Sweat ran down my sides, my back, my forehead. I brushed it out of my eyes remembering not to look at the hideous flames. If I did, I'd never leave this place.

More to get away from the blasted lake than anything, I plodded along the line, careful not to touch it. I got maybe a hundred meters before I ran into a solid rock wall. Was it illusion? I probed this way and that but couldn't tell.

Next, I retraced my steps only to run into a similar phenomenon beyond the other end of the lake. I'd barely made it past the lake this time before a cliff barred further progress. The lake's magnetism was growing; it took every scrap of self-discipline to not stop and lose myself in the play of fire and color above its restless surface.

I was wasting valuable time. And limited magic. Charon's words about this place leaving its mark on me blazed as bright as the fire-choked water.

"Don't think about what he said," I growled.

Raising my hands, I tested the integrity of the rock blocking my path. It was solid. So solid I wasn't at all certain I could jump through it, magic or no.

I stared at the pulsing ley line. Surely, I hadn't come all this way to turn back. I have my faults, but I'm no quitter. The line slithered through the wall, but there was no room for anything beyond its bulk.

Or was there?

An idea battered me, one so absurd and risky, no one but a fool would do anything but turn back. Still, it was the only way. Charon had shown me this spot for a reason. For all I knew, it was the only place someone like me could locate the lines.

Merging with them was my only option. If I did, would I be able to reverse the process? Or would my energy be absorbed and become part of the ley lines forever?

I stared at the line, tapped it tentatively with my power, and recoiled. As if it had been awaiting my touch, it almost nabbed me. Even with a tiny touch, I'd barely escaped its pull.

The lines were as mesmerizing as the lake. Either I did this, or I had to leave pronto. While I still could.

The energy pulsing from the lines shifted. Even absent words, I sensed their deep displeasure at my possible departure. It should have terrified me, but I was tired and done playing games.

"You want me so much?" I shouted. "Then take me."

Rather than me stepping forward, or doing anything at all, the line reared up, wrapped around me, and sucked me inside.

Too shocked to struggle against its pull, I buckled in for the ride. The lines were warm, comforting, soothing. The parents and friends I'd never had. Voices crooned to me, reassured me I could have it all. Everything I've ever wanted.

Truth crashed over me as the lines shot me forward. They knew they were injured. I was the only one who could repair the breach. Even if I'd made a different choice as I stood looking at them, they'd never have allowed me to leave.

Other times in my life have felt like that. Where my choices were made for me. I just hoped at the far end of this —if there was such a thing—I wouldn't be so changed I'd lose everything I loved and valued.

The voices escalated. They *were* everything. They'd give me everything. No more worries, ever. I was theirs. They'd awaited my arrival forever.

I filed it all away. I'd fix the damned lines, but then I'd make it clear I was done. We'd see how the outcome of that tiny piece of rebellion played out. Charon had known. He must have. It was why he'd warned me.

Just like always, at the end of the day, I had only myself to blame—and to fall back on. It should have been comforting, but I was holding myself together by the barest of margins. I'd given up control of my destiny.

For now, but not forever.

Clinging to that thought, I catapulted forward encased in the lines. There had to be a way out.

Had to be.

CHAPTER 19

BLAKE

"What do you mean she went in search of the lines by herself?" I thundered while swatting at Hedrek. It was absurd since he flew out of reach easily.

"Why didn't she wait for us?" Roya asked the owl.

"I told her not to," Hedrek replied. "She had an opportunity, one which might have dwindled had she tarried."

"And you knew this, how?" I snarled.

Fuck. I was beyond furious. Beyond everything. Abria, my Abria, had ridden into danger by herself. My brave, foolish darling.

Give it a break, a wise inner part of me instructed dryly.

Brave, yes. My darling, also yes. Foolish, never. She'd escaped Satan's clutches on her own. Being a drama king would put me in the same camp as the Cait and a whole lot of other mages I've always looked down on.

"I'm going after her," I told Roya and the owl. Before they could protest, I added, "Alone."

"You have to take me." Roya crossed her arms beneath her breasts.

"I go where I please," Hedrek informed my loftily.

"True enough," I told him. "But your presence could complicate things."

"I fail to see how." He clacked his beak twice and vanished in a shower of bluish sparks.

Great. I'd alienated him, and now he was off on his own. My leadership skills were slipping badly. Part of my team was in the wind.

"Let's go," Roya urged. "Time's getting away from us."

I turned toward her. "Why do you want to do this? Someone has to remain here to watch over Abel and Marika."

The changeling frowned. "Hedrek promised Abria he'd do that. I saw it in his mind."

I sure as hell hadn't, but then I hadn't been looking. I'd been so spun out about her being gone, I wasn't doing much but overreacting all over the place.

"Do you know where Abria went?" I leveled my gaze at Roya.

She glanced away. "Maybe. Not for sure."

"Show me."

Imagery flooded my mind. Places I hadn't seen for many a long year. "Hell? She returned to Hell?" I gritted.

Roya nodded, her pointed chin bobbing. "It's the only way to find the ley lines."

"Why are you so sure?"

"I heard others talking about them in the *Dreaming*. Abria isn't the first to seek them out." She hesitated, gaze glued to the ground.

"What aren't you saying?"

"Mages who've seen the lines are...altered. It's why they opted for the *Dreaming*. They were incapable of functioning in their former lives."

News to me. No one had ever mentioned a problem with the lines before. Even when they were in tiptop shape, and we'd taken their contribution to our magic for granted.

"We should leave," Roya repeated.

"Look at me."

She scraped her gaze up off the ground. Worry filled her dark eyes, and the skin around them was pinched into many tiny lines.

I dropped a hand onto her bony shoulder. "One of us must remain to care for the cats. It cannot be me."

The shoulder beneath my grip slumped. "I understand. Where would you have me take them if something bad happens?"

"By then, it will be too late. You must observe carefully. At the first whiff they've been discovered—or are in any kind of trouble—hustle them to Underhill. Doesn't matter which part. They'll be safe there until my return."

"I understand and will obey."

Her formalized response surprised me. "Thank you for accepting my direction."

She ducked from under my hand and bowed low. "I am Sidhe. You made me such and are my liege."

"Still, I appreciate your compliance." I didn't bother to

add that those who actually obeyed me were a minority these days.

We'd settled on a course of action. "I'll be back as soon as I can," I told her. Summoning enough enchantment to move me from here to what I hoped was an unobtrusive corner of Hell, I left Roya to her assigned task.

I should have been gone the moment I knew Abria had taken matters into her own hands. Instead, I'd spent the better part of half an hour between Hedrek and Roya.

Couldn't be helped. If I hadn't taken the time, Roya would have run off half-cocked just like Hedrek. And then I'd have had to pull Abel and Marika away from their posts to free myself to go after Abria.

The cats were in a useful position. So far, no one suspected what they were about. It would have been a shame to remove them after all the trouble we'd gone to getting them into place.

I felt responsible for them, and I couldn't leave them to fend for themselves. How would Hedrek explain his dereliction of duty to Abria? As if it mattered. Their relationship wasn't my problem.

For all I knew, he had some way of watching over them from wherever he'd run off to.

My mind was all over the place as my spell spit me out in absolute darkness. The characteristic rotten stench of Hell assaulted my nostrils. My stomach twisted sourly as I sorted decaying vegetation from decomposing flesh. When this was over, it would be a while before my appetite returned.

I started forward, intent on locating the ley lines. If I

could find them, I'd find Abria. Something blocked my path. I tried working around it by feel.

No go.

Reluctantly, I kindled a sliver of a mage light. Not much shocks me, but I was surrounded by corpses and piles of garbage. The thing I'd tripped over was an enormous carcass. Perhaps a rhinoceros, but it was too badly decomposed to know for sure. If it had horns, someone had stripped them. Satan's never run a particularly tight ship, but this was waste pure and simple.

Since when did Hell's sovereign allow perfectly good meat to rot on the bones?

Heh. He probably doesn't know about it.

I picked my way around bodies that had been tossed on heaps of decomposing vegetation. A light touch brushed my mind, followed by something more distinctive.

Earth had found me.

Crap. Was she going to chide me for the Cait fiasco again?

"I know you're there," I informed her. *"Where are the ley lines? You could save me a lot of time."*

A breath of fresher air wafted past me. I followed it across the vast chamber and out into a drafty hall. Avoiding detection was high on my list. Satan and I weren't exactly on cordial terms. Still, I moved faster when I wasn't feeling my way forward. Navigating with magic is even more of a dead giveaway than my light, so I kept it engaged but dialed low.

I wanted to ask Earth if she knew where Abria was, but didn't. She could be possessive, believing that as emissary for the Sidhe, I belonged to her. We benefit greatly from our connection with the natural world, but it's never made me her lackey, no matter how she perceives things.

The air channel led me lower and then lower still. I overtook the occasional demon, but I was well warded and passed unnoticed. The sound of distant squabbles ebbed and flowed. Arguments about food, space, whose orders superseded someone else's. My grasp of demonspeak is rudimentary at best; I'm sure I missed a lot in translation.

Most of my attention was focused on avoiding detection. I trusted Earth to keep her side of the bargain we hadn't exactly made and lead me to Abria. Because I wasn't paying close attention, I very nearly fell into a shaft. The puffs of air I'd been following vanished into a hole in damp ground.

The opening was just big enough for me to fit through. Unless the shaft opened below, this would be a one-way trip since there wasn't room for me to turn around. Dirt scuttled into the pit. I took a step back in case the whole structure chose this moment to collapse.

Earth was nowhere near. My choices were few. Follow her into the pit or strike out on my own. Presumably, Hedrek was down here. He might be having better luck than me—or at least a more direct route to Abria. I sent power zinging along the link I have with her. It was how I'd planned to find her in the first place before Earth stepped in.

I followed the bit of magic. Followed it. Followed it. All of a sudden, it boomeranged back and punched me in the guts so hard I doubled over. *Oof.* I rubbed my tender stomach and straightened.

That avenue wouldn't work. I've never had issues with

my enchantment misbehaving in the upper levels of Hell before. Why now?

When I searched for the hole, it was closing at an alarming rate. I could be left here with nothing and no way to help Abria. I hadn't cared for the specter of jumping into a foreign space.

Who knew where it went? Aye, and who cared? Control could be my middle name, but clinging to the helm of a sinking ship was absurd.

"Doesn't matter," I muttered and stuffed my feet into the opening. My shoulders got stuck. It took some maneuvering to free up space to allow me to navigate the fast-disappearing passageway.

I barked a power word, followed by two more instructing the channel to hold its current form until I was through. It seemed to do the trick. I still felt as if I was being squeezed through the belly of a python, but at least I didn't require additional magic to slow my descent.

It grew warmer exponentially as I descended. Sweat slicked my back and sides and oozed into my eyes. I blinked, but it made the stinging worse. Corralling bits of free magic, I searched for Abria again.

My tracking spell didn't bounce back and slap me this time, but neither did it pinpoint her location. If Abria was anywhere down here, she must be heavily warded or—

I chopped that thought off fast. If she'd been captured again, Satan and his princes were more than capable of building magic-proof shielding around her. I might not be able to reach Abria, but could I communicate with the Sidhe in case I required assistance?

The bottom rose up to meet me as I searched for Kirwan and Breanne. Still feet down, I bent my knees to take up the shock of landing. The minute my feet touched something solid, my transit channel crackled around me and turned to a gray mist.

My breath came quick in the extreme heat. Now that my arms weren't pinned next to my sides, I swiped a forearm across my damp forehead and hunted for the billow of fresh air I'd been following.

"*Took you long enough,*" Earth groused.

I decided not to answer. The truth would piss her off, and she'd sniff out a lie. I also didn't apologize. It's a sign of weakness.

"*Walk fifty paces ahead,*" Earth instructed.

"Where will you be?" I asked, suddenly suspicious.

"*Elsewhere. My task is done.*"

She wasn't kidding. Her withdrawal from my mind was abrupt, leaving an empty space. I refused to grovel and beg her to stay. Kirwan hadn't answered. Neither had Breanne.

Fifty paces ahead, huh? I brightened my mage light and glanced at my surroundings. If it hadn't been so ungodly hot, this place held an eldritch beauty. Huge crystals dotted the walls, sticking out at odd angles. My light reflected off them. The ground was clear of debris, almost as if someone tended it. I caught a whiff of steam, suggesting an underground pool wasn't far off.

Holding my position—so I'd get the dead ahead part right—I strode the requisite fifty paces and ended up on the rim of a shallow pit. Running along the bottom were the ley lines. Two of them, each as big around as my thigh.

I picked my way into the trench. As I got closer, I saw the source of the steam. An underground river flowed behind the lines, chittering over rocks. A fine mist rose, mirroring colors like a prism. For a time, I stared at the vista laid out before me. It promised peace, solace, a safe place to while away forever.

And then, I wised up.

If I weren't careful, I'd end up glued to this spot for eternity, lost in the interplay of light and water. Building protections took far longer than I expected. Once they were in place, I crouched next to the lines and let my hands hover over them.

I knew better than to touch their outer shells. The energy would be more than enough to fry me. Something familiar teased the edges of my mind. I moved a hand closer until it hovered right above where the two lines touched.

"Blake!" burst into my mind, staggering me so I fell backward onto my ass.

"Abria?" I held my breath. Had I found her only to lose her again?

"Yes. I'm stuck in the lines. They're fixed, but I can't get out. They won't let me go."

Fuck. Oh holy godhead.

Sweat poured into my eyes. I ignored it. My hand that had hovered over the lines settled briefly. Searing pain roared up my arm. The lines protected their own.

"Blake?" Hopelessness ran beneath the one word.

"We'll figure something out." I tried to sound positive, upbeat, but she knows me, and I couldn't erase every trace of worry.

"You should leave."

"Never. I am not leaving you." I got my feet under me and stood.

The swoosh of feathers dragged my head around. "Finally got here, eh?" the owl hooted.

I didn't dignify his commentary with a response. Instead, I asked, "Where have you been?"

"Where else? Trying to find a solution."

I stared at the owl. "And?"

He clacked his beak once and then again. "Not looking good."

"Leave, both of you," Abria cried.

I didn't bother with telepathy since she could hear us. "I can't speak for Hedrek," I said, "but I'm not going anywhere."

The owl hooted mournfully. I walked the length of the lines until I hit a wall. There had to be a way out of this. Had to be. I needed my library, but I wouldn't abandon Abria. Not for one second.

"There is one thing we could try," Hedrek spoke deep into my mind. I had no idea if Abria could hear him.

"Tell me," I used equally shielded mind speech and took stock of my magic. I'd need every shred before this was done. The lines are the source of my power—and every other magic wielder's. If I had to engage in a pitched battle with them, it could drain my skill so fast I'd be left with nothing.

Don't think like that.

The owl nudged me with his beak and began to talk.

CHAPTER 20

ABRIA

Repairing the lines had been anticlimactic, trivial. Apparently, they'd once been split into two. Something about my making had merged them. All I'd had to do was carve notches in a few strategic places from my special vantage spot within. The lines had moaned, sounding like a woman on the brink of release. Emotions raced through me where I was linked with them. Joy. Relief. Gratitude.

Not my feelings, but the lines were using me as a sounding board. Maybe they were testing how firmly I was snared. I'd never know. Not wanting to get caught up in their delight at returning to their original configuration, I shielded myself as best I could.

The whole process couldn't have taken more than half an hour.

And then the interesting part began.

I started with a straightforward approach. "I helped you. You're whole. Now free me."

Raucous laughter replaced the sensual moans. It annoyed the crap out of me. My next gambit was more direct. "I did as you wished. Release me this instant."

"Nay, little mage. You belong to us. The Celts made you for us. And then they reneged on the bargain. They claimed you ran away, but they could have found you. We were watching. They didn't even try."

Fury carved a track through me. Goddess damn the Celts for all eternity. Arianrhod might have mentioned their agreement with the lines. Perhaps she'd have gotten around to it—offering her the benefit of the doubt—but I didn't think so. If she was ashamed by how I'd turned out, she must have been doubly chagrined at owing the ley lines anything.

"What exactly did you give the Celts in return?" I asked sweetly. So long as I was stuck here, a captive audience, I may as well gather every scrap of information I could.

The nasty laugh was back. "Greedy bunch, those Celtic gods," the lines hissed.

Not an answer, but I could afford to be patient. So I waited.

A high-pitched buzzing was followed by, "The promise was they would maintain their position of sovereignty."

Certainly not the reply I was expecting. I'd had no idea their top-of-the-heap status was in jeopardy. Even more concerning was they'd created me for totally selfish reasons. Not that it came as a surprise. They'd always been a greedy pack of self-serving jerks.

"What will you gain by forcing me to remain?" I tried another tack.

"You are ours, created with our energy," Multiple voices chimed together. "You have always been ours. Your rightful place is here."

I squeezed my eyes shut. Or thought I did. Did I still have a body? It was impossible to tell. "My rightful place"—I spoke slowly—"is with the animals and birds and fish. I was created to help them, be their advocate."

"Eh, they'll get along without you."

Alrighty. I wasn't going to argue my way out of this. No reason to waste breath. The lines were convinced I belonged to them. If they assumed I was going to capitulate without causing them as much grief as I could, they were dead wrong.

I took stock of my magic, gratified to discover it was limitless. Ha. Guess the lines couldn't hang onto me and cut me off from their bounty at the same time. Good to know.

Could they read my mind? Best to assume so. After all, they'd subsumed me into the flow of their enchantment. Still, I had to lay out my options and pick the most promising escape hatch. Nothing would work if they knew what I was going to do before I launched it.

I withdrew into myself, building the strongest shell I could. No one laughed at me. Maybe the lines had moved on. Confident I was theirs forever, they no longer needed to pay attention to me.

Yeah, a girl can wish for miracles...

I explored my dilemma from every angle. It wasn't easy since panic rode near the surface. Being stuck here would be a whole lot like being dead. My ongoing analysis showed a single path that might work. I'd have to turn their magic against them. A risky maneuver. They're the source of my power. I'd have to be stealthy and quick. If they cut me off, I'd have displayed my hand and gotten nowhere.

And I'd never get a second chance. They might not be able to curb my flow of magic, but they'd make damn sure I couldn't direct it against them.

Waiting was my best strategy. Let the lines grow complacent believing I'd adjusted to my fate. After all, they didn't view my problem as a problem at all. The lines saw themselves as the end-all and be-all. They'd bestowed a great honor upon me by joining their power with mine.

If I hadn't been trapped, my head would have snapped up. Maybe they weren't as powerful as all that. They'd needed me to fix their architecture, make them whole again. If they'd required me for that, I bet there were many flaws in their structure. All I had to do was pinpoint them.

I was sunk in testing the nearby segment of line for weakness when I felt Hedrek's energy. Would the lines notice the owl? So far, there wasn't any evidence they had. I felt him moving this way and that. If I modulated my third eye, I could see him through the translucent coating over the lines.

I wanted to talk with him, but didn't.

Mages probably visited the ley lines from time to time. No reason to alert them about this particular visitor. Our power has always slotted well together. If we worked as a team, maybe he'd provide the added ingredient that could spring me.

I retreated to hunting for vulnerabilities in the lines' makeup. Hedrek had moved out of visual range, but then Blake showed up.

Damn it all to Hell and back. I could get myself out of this. If he'd ridden in like some medieval knight intent on doing something flashy—which would put him at risk—to save me, I'd never forgive him.

Especially not if his master plan involved trading his freedom for my own.

I'd hidden Hedrek's link with me, but the owl was canny enough not to get caught. Blinded by his love for me, Blake was sure to do something ill advised.

"Blake!" His name tore out of me.

"Abria?" He sounded momentarily confused.

"Yes. I'm stuck in the lines. They're fixed, but I can't get out. They won't let me go."

I felt a disturbance when he grabbed the line. It took everything in me not to shriek at him. Surely, he, a Sidhe prince, knew better than to touch the source of his power.

Instead, I simply said his name again. *"Blake?"*

"We'll figure something out." He tried to sound positive, upbeat, but I knew him, and he was plenty worried.

"You should leave." I tried for firm.

"Never. I am not leaving you."

Of course, I'd known as much. Stubborn as the day was long, my Daoine Sidhe prince. Hedrek waltzed back in. I had no trouble hearing them absent mind speech. But then all of a sudden, I couldn't. I wove power this way and that, but couldn't penetrate whatever type of sound shield they'd woven around each another.

I didn't need to hear to know they were planning my escape, at grave risk to themselves. No help for it. I had to break myself out of the lines—and damned quickly.

Brilliant ideas are like falling stars—you have to get a jump on them, or they fritter to sparks of nothingness. This idea was simplicity itself. The lines had needed me to mend them, but what I'd mended I could break. Then I'd have leverage.

I'd promise to redo my repairs, but only if they made an unshakeable vow to let me go afterward. Since I was one with the lines, I visualized the precise spots where I needed to strike.

And then I moved fast. Damned fast. There were six places to address. Remember, I said my fix-it task bordered on the anticlimactic. I'd rebroken four of them before an iron grip circled my waist.

"What do you think you're doing?" Hostility skewered the words together.

Talk about rhetorical questions. "What does it look like I'm doing?" I replied all saccharine and innocence, not bothering with telepathy. On the heels of my response, I felt the lines merging, taking the configuration that had caused everyone so much angst and been the source of other mages hating me.

Yes! I'd have fist pumped the air if my arms had been free. Perhaps I didn't have to break all six places again. Four seemed to have done the trick.

"Return them to their original configuration," thundered through my head.

I beat back a victorious smile. I'd been right. This meant

a lot to the lines. "Of course," I agreed quickly. Too quickly. "On one condition."

"*We do not bargain with mages,*" the voice informed me haughtily.

"Then I guess you're shit out of luck." I held my breath. Had I pushed it too far?

The grip around my waist tightened once more, reminding me of steel pincers cutting into my flesh. "Fine," I gasped while I still had air to talk. "Kill me, and no one will ever fix you. It must be me, or you wouldn't have waited all this time for unity."

Or in this case, duality, but I wasn't in the mood to split hairs.

"Ooph. You're hurting me," I ground out.

The arm—or whatever it was—squeezed tighter. My visual field turned to a haze of red dots.

I held my ground. Either I won this war, or I'd perish trying. If they could actually kill me. I'm immortal, so I wasn't sure they could inflict permanent damage.

I'd lost track of Hedrek and Blake. Neither could enter the lines.

Thank all the gods for small favors.

My head spun. I'd have puked if there'd been anything in my stomach and the pressure had been a little less. It was blocking my windpipe and esophagus.

"*You little bitch. Fix this.*"

We were there. Rubber-meets-road time. "Sure, but you must give me your solemn word you will let me go afterward."

I waited for another lecture about not bargaining with

mages. It never came. The hideous pressure on my midsection vanished as quickly as it had come. I sucked air like a bellows and hurried to dismantle the last two places I'd repaired.

May as well make a clean break of everything.

I heard an odd sound. It took a moment before I realized it was me laughing. Not only laughing, roaring with mirth. Even if they tossed me in a dungeon somewhere, I'd won this round.

Familiar magic encompassed me, dragged me from the line where I'd been encased. Before I had a chance to say anything, Blake and Hedrek launched a journey spell. The cavern with the river and the lines disappeared.

"Don't know how far we'll get," Blake muttered.

"Sure you do," the owl countered about the time their casting crashed and burned dumping us out in darkness.

I tried for a mage light, but its glow was pathetic.

"What did you do to piss them off?" Blake asked me.

"Me?" Hoping I sounded like the soul of innocence, I shrugged. "How do you know they're not retaliating against you? After all, you're who dragged me out of the lines."

"Because something changed right before our rescue," Hedrek explained. "We had everything planned out, but then the lines merged into a single entity."

"How did that happen?" Blake prodded me.

"There was only one line before I intervened. No one was more surprised than me when my fix-it job split it into two."

"That was their original configuration," Blake murmured, "but it still doesn't explain how they ended up one line again."

I undid my work," I admitted. "Planned to use it as a bargaining chip to force them to release me, but I never had the chance to see if it would have panned out."

My feet were on solid ground, but I couldn't see very well. "Where are we?"

"Still in Hell, unfortunately," Blake replied.

"How'd you untangle me from the lines?"

"It was Hedrek's idea," Blake said.

"I wasn't certain it would work," the owl admitted, "but we amplified Blake's link with you and poured pure fire along its path. The flames opened a channel. Pulling you through was straightforward probably because the lines weren't expecting that approach."

"Creative. Thank you."

"You're most welcome," Hedrek hooted, "but I couldn't have pulled it off without Blake's power. Fire is far from my favored element.

I'd have smiled if I wasn't so wiped out.

My take-home lesson du jour: the simplest solution is usually best. While I was tucking that tidbit away, my mage light guttered and died. With a sinking feeling I tested the rest of my power. Not much left.

"Not fond of this solution, but I need to go back," I told them.

"Over my dead body." Blake draped a possessive arm around my shoulders.

I ducked from beneath his embrace and spread my hands in front of me. "If I don't reconfigure the lines, none of us will ever be able to access our magic again."

"You can't know that," Blake protested.

"Yeah, I can. They're furious. Before you stepped in, they were only angry with me, but it wouldn't surprise me if the lines extended their moratorium on power to every Sidhe."

"They wouldn't dare." Blake shook a fist.

"I wouldn't put it past them," Hedrek hooted.

Even more reason for me to suck it up and repeat my repair on the lines. My idea held risks, big ones. No matter what I did, the lines might not reinstitute our connection with their power. We could probably walk out of Hell from our current position, although I wasn't certain of that. An ill-timed demon attack could prove disastrous since we'd have no magic to counteract theirs.

"If I don't do this," I argued, "we'll sink into a no-man's land where we're no longer mages." The specter of losing my connection to the animal world sent a shiver down my back—a neat trick in the ever-present heat of the nether realm. I wasn't sure I wanted to continue absent the animals, birds, insects, and fish that had filled my life almost since my creation.

"Whatever happens, we're all in this together," Blake announced.

"Aye, I promised Arianrhod I'd keep a close eye on you," Hedrek hooted.

He meant well, but it was the wrong thing to say. I rounded on the hapless owl. "The Celts created me as part of a bargain with the ley lines. Did you know that?"

His round eyes might have opened even wider. Tough to tell in the murky light where we'd ended up. "I did not," was followed by a couple of indignant squawks.

"What kind of bargain?" Blake demanded.

"They'd maintain their status at the tip-top of the mage hierarchy. In return, they'd hand me over to the lines as some sort of perpetual guardian."

"Why, those slimy bastards. I'd like to—"

"Not now," I cut in. I'd been considering how best to approach the ley lines for my second go-round. Honey buys more than vinegar. I could see it from the ley lines' point of view. They'd made a bargain in good faith. Never mind it planted me dead center as an indentured servant. They didn't think in those terms. I was a means to an end: perpetuation of their integrity. Nothing more, or less.

"You are not going back alone." Blake's tone was emphatic.

"Aye. How do you know they won't trap you the same way they did before?" Hedrek tossed out.

"I trapped myself," I informed them. "Entered the lines willingly because I wasn't getting anywhere outside them. I had no idea it would even work, but I no sooner thought about joining with them than I slid into their midst. I had no idea it would be a one-way trip."

I shook my head. "We're wasting time. I'm leaving."

"How?" Blake countered. "Your magic is just as dead as ours."

I offered a crooked smile. "If I open my mind to the ley lines, tell them I wish to return, they'll finesse my journey."

"While you're at it, tell them to include us," Blake said dryly.

It didn't seem like a good idea, but neither did I want to leave them here. Visualizing the spot Blake and Hedrek had dragged me from the lines, I formulated an open-ended agreement.

"I will repair you from the outside in but only if you agree to me leaving afterward. My companions must accompany me."

Blake wound a hand around my upper arm. Hedrek perched with a foot on each of my shoulders. Clearly, they weren't taking any chances of me slipping away without them. Absent their own magic, there wasn't much they could do if the lines sorted my essence from theirs and spirited me away, but I'd said my piece.

Minutes slipped by, one after another. Just when I was certain the ley lines had jettisoned me for good, considering me too much trouble, the place we stood flooded with pale-yellow glow. Enchantment buzzed around us, the ground opened, and we tumbled downward.

CHAPTER 21

ABRIA

Hedrek's talons tore tracks in my shoulders as he struggled to hang on. It was a losing battle since there wasn't space to spread his wings. The scent of my blood thickened around me. I worked feverishly to close the wounds with the very last of my magic. Blood would give the lines power over me. Maybe enough to snare me forever. Blake was forced from my side almost immediately since the chasm we fell through was narrow.

Was the lines' strategy to divide and conquer?

I'd find out soon enough. Blood reek lingered, but I'd sealed my injured places. Swallowing was tough; my stomach twisted into a sour knot. Maybe this hadn't been one of my better ideas, but it wasn't as if I'd had a choice. I had to reclaim my power. And I'd never have forgiven myself if the ley lines isolated the Sidhe from their magic on my account. I had a feeling Hedrek would land on his talons either way, since he and Arianrhod were on a first name basis.

Or something.

I plummeted end over end. Normally, I'd have called on my skill to right myself—but my reservoir was bone-dry. I fell through darkness, unable to sense Blake or the owl.

Fool's errand, an inner voice shrieked.

Shut up, I answered myself and imagined crashing into goddess-only-knew-what at the bottom.

There had to be a bottom, but we fell so long I was beginning to wonder. Finally, finally, after I'd cursed my stupidity nine ways from Faery, my headlong trajectory first slowed and then stopped. The infernal darkness ceded to a soft white light. I floated, before landing gently on sand next to the ley lines.

"You belong to us," roared through my head.

Not a time to show weakness. I stood tall, shoulders rolled back, and pushed tangled hair out of my face. "I belong to no one but myself," I replied, and then hurried to add, "I understand you made a deal with the Celts, but they had no right to sell me into slavery—to anyone."

"But they made you with our energies." The voice changed timbre, turning silky smooth.

"'Tisn't slavery," another voice chimed in, *"but a great honor."*

Aha! I'd been right about that part. Blake plopped down on one side of me, Hedrek on the other. Before either had a chance to gather their wits, I forged ahead. "I appreciate the honor of being an integral part of the ley lines. You are ancient, forged in the very makings of all worlds."

I stopped to take in a breath and chose a direction. What I said next would make or break my attempt to recoup all our power. Small sighs rustled around me. What I'd stated so far hadn't pissed them off.

Rather than me telling them what I wanted, I took a chance and asked, "How can we work together in ways that offer us both freedom? I will commit to being here whenever there are problems with the lines."

I stopped there. Would my proposal be met with consideration—or derision? Before, they'd assumed if I wasn't a captive audience I wouldn't be there at all.

Blake moved between me and the glowing line. Bowing low, he spoke in the eldritch language of the Sidhe. I only caught one word out of perhaps three, but the gist of what he said was, "The Sidhe, my people, are grateful for your everlasting presence—"

"How would we know that? You have led the Sidhe for millennia. In all that time, we have seen you a grand total of twice. And both times you wanted something."

Blake flinched—a slight movement, but I noticed—and bowed again. "You are correct. Please accept my apologies. I vow to do better."

Muttered phrases about talk being cheap eddied around me. They didn't say it like that, but it was what they meant.

"What can I do to redeem myself?" Blake's question held formal tones.

"Only time will provide redemption."

"Fair enough," he agreed. Despite him facing away from me, I could almost see his brain whirling into overdrive. He's always been more of a big-picture person than me. Where was he was going with this?

Rather than waiting for him to divert the ley lines, I stepped to his side. "For my part," I said, "I will either come as soon as I can if you need me, or we can set a schedule."

"No need to call you," one voice murmured.

"You are part of us," another cut in.

Charon's prediction about the lines altering me sprang to the fore. "In what way?" I sought clarification.

"You will see."

Annoyance scoured me, leaving a bitter taste in my mouth. "Not good enough. If I'm already 'part of you,' why the need to hold me against my will?"

Where I stared at the line, it shimmered and glistened, growing harder and harder to look at. Blake hooked a hand around my upper arm as he stared at the growing coruscation.

Hedrek had been silent but started hooting excitedly. Did he and Blake know something that was eluding me?

The glow brightened until I shielded my eyes. When it cleared, a woman stood on the far side of the line, old-fashioned lantern in hand. Cream-colored robes draped her tall, slender form, falling to the ground. A crimson sash spanned her waist. Acres of silver hair curled around her face and shoulders, cascading to waist level and below. Her eyes were a collection of constantly moving images. Were it not for them, she'd have appeared preternaturally young, perhaps not more than sixteen.

I knew better. Plus, she reeked of Celtic magic.

Blake shook a fist. "Bodhmall. Were you in on this all along?"

Bodhmall? Who in the hell was she? I racked my brain until I recalled she'd been a fairly minor deity only remembered because she was Fionn MacCumhaill's aunt. He'd been a seer, poet, and quite the hero in Irish folklore. Were it not for him, her name would have faded from memory.

Laughter filled the cavern. "Nice to see you too, Elwyn Cardassier. 'Tis been a while." She turned her attention on me.

"Do you not wish to come home, child?"

It was concealed, but I recognized compulsion beneath her words. I fought to keep the word *yes* safely in the confines of my mouth. "This will never be my home," I gritted. "And stop calling me child."

"But, child, you were formed with stuff from these lines. How else do you think we breathed life into you?"

Her persistent use of child grated. But who had the "we" part been? Apparently more than Arianrhod, Ceridwen, and the Morrigan.

Blake picked up on it too. "You were part of the plot around Abria's making," he accused.

She batted a hand his way as if he were the slightest of nuisances. "Quiet, Sidhe."

Blake inserted his body between me and Bodhmall. Didn't slow her down at all. She jumped the line and materialized on my other side. Hedrek chose that moment to waddle up to her.

"It won't work," the owl noted.

"Why not?" Bodhmall demanded.

"What won't work?" I hustled to get a couple of words in edgewise.

"Abria doesn't want to be here," the owl continued, ignoring me. "Eventually, her discontent will pollute the lines, and you'll be worse off than you are now." He clacked his beak. "Let her reestablish their dual nature, and then release her. It's the only way."

"I didn't wish to be here, either," the goddess pointed out. "Yet here I am."

The pieces were falling into place even absent an explanation. "You thought to trade my freedom for your own?" My voice edged higher, but I restrained myself from tacking "how dare you?" onto the end of my statement.

"Now it's coming back to me," Blake muttered. "The Celts created the ley lines to augment their power, but they were never able to keep other mages from tapping into them. It was always a point of contention. If I recall, they lost control of the lines altogether."

Bodhmall extended an arm, index finger pointing at Blake. "Quiet, Sidhe. I warned you once."

He shook his head. "Or what? Nay, I will not be quiet. For some reason, that bit of knowledge was concealed. I knew it once but lost sight of it."

"Because the Celts wished it so," Hedrek explained.

The owl knew a lot. Too bad he hadn't been more forthcoming with information. Maybe spells had stilled his tongue—or loyalty to Arianrhod.

At least I understood why they'd bothered with me in the first place. I was designed as a stand-in to babysit the ley lines. "Why couldn't you repair the lines without me?" I asked the goddess.

"Only you can make them whole," she retorted. "'Tis the energy you're made with." Her eyes widened; she glared at Hedrek. "What did you do, bird?"

"Made certain you spoke true."

Handy trick. I nodded at the owl who'd befriended me. Never mind it had been at Arianrhod's behest; he was still on my side.

I twisted until I faced Bodhmall. "This is why I've been hunted, isn't it? You and your kin expected you could force me back to the lines. So you spread rumors far and wide among mages. Tales I was to blame for their fading ability."

"This is your rightful place. One you've avoided far too long."

Breath hissed from between my clenched teeth. "You make it sound like I'm long-lost royalty with a throne to collect." I shook my head. "None of that matters. I'll keep my word, establish the lines' inherent duality, and then Blake, Hedrek, and I are leaving."

"I think not." After uttering an ear-splitting howl, Bodhmall dove at me, her face contorted with fury. I ducked, but she caught one side of my face with her long nails. She had power; I didn't. But I punched and bit and tangled my fists in her long hair pulling as hard as I could. If she thought she could bodily drag me back inside the lines, I wouldn't go easily.

Hisses and shrieks filled the air, along with grunts and pants. I tasted blood, not sure if it was mine or hers. She pulled my hair so hard my scalp felt as if it were on fire.

Blake threw himself at her back and was doing his damnedest to pull her off me. Hedrek flew this way and that meting out damage with his hooked beak.

Bodhmall's will bore down on me, surrounding my brain and threatening to crush the very life out of me. The pressure was huge, excruciating. Along with it, she hummed hypnotic bits of sound. Between the two, I was sinking, losing ground no matter what I did.

With the last of my free will—because that was what she was after—I opened a corner of my power-depleted essence to the lines, not expecting much. If anything, it could have made my situation worse since the lines could have sucked me right back in.

Maybe. It might have taken the goddess-presence to accomplish that. Or not. The first time, I'd merged with them willingly.

Hedrek and Blake were fading from my consciousness. They were there, but reality had turned dreamlike, kaleidoscopic. Even the pain Bodhmall meted out had developed a muted quality. The copper-sweet smell of blood was everywhere. Some of it hers, but mostly mine.

If I was on my way out, I would not go quietly. If the fucking lines absorbed me, they'd have to take her too. With both hands grasping her hair, I called to the lines. Magic flooded me, hot, fresh, unexpected. I sent bolts of lightning to the spots the goddess clung to me.

Still shrieking like a madwoman, she let go as if she'd been burned. Large areas of charred flesh and the scent of roasting meat suggested I'd done precisely that. Breath rasped in my throat as I kept a close eye on her. I expected her to retaliate. When she didn't, victory surged—and knowledge.

I was stronger than she was. Strong enough she leapt over the line and glared balefully at me from a distance.

Maybe I was more formidable than any of the Celts. Mixed blood confers advantages. No wonder none of them were forthcoming about my beginnings. Wasn't it just too convenient to sequester me inside the lines where my magic would only manifest behind the scenes?

No more. I'd rise above all this, above them, and make the lines my own.

I opened my mouth, intent on staking a claim, my claim, to the lines' power. I'd control it, dole it out, make everyone who'd ever hunted me sorry they'd been born.

"Watch it, Abria," Blake shouted. "You do not want to do this. Anything we claim becomes ours. The lines belong to every mage, not only you. Assuming ownership was where the Celts made one of many catastrophic errors."

His words were like a bucket of ice water. Thank the gods he lived in my head and anticipated my moves. I may want their magic, but I did not want to own them. They belonged to all of us.

What in the hell had happened to me? I focused on the goddess standing a few meters away with the line between us.

Her mouth twisted in fury, and she turned aside. She'd planted those seeds. The ones where I'd choke on my own greed and revenge and fall into the very trap the Celts had laid for me long ago.

'Thanks," I called to Blake.

He gave me one of his famous pointed glances but didn't follow it up with an I-told-you-so. Or worse, a how-could-you-be-such-a-dimwit?

Enchantment from the lines flowed strongly. I followed it and tapped the places I'd undone earlier. The single line obligingly split into two. A satisfied sigh rustled through my head.

I nodded and dusted my hands together. "There. Everything is back to normal."

My words might have been prophetic. Streamers of light sprang from the lines and wound around Bodhmall. When they vanished, so did she. Presumably back within the ley lines.

A spell bubbled around Blake. "My magic is back! Time for us to leave," he said.

I shook my head. "Not quite yet." Walking next to the lines, I sank into a crouch. "If you ever have need of me, reach for me. I will come."

The nearest line brightened. I took it as a sign I'd been heard.

As soon as I joined Blake and the owl, the cavern shattered replaced by blackness. "Beats walking," he joked.

"Not flying," the owl observed.

"Where are we going?" I asked.

"Back to where I left Roya, Abel, and Marika," Blake replied.

I winced. Of course, we'd want to bring them with us. No longer fighting for my freedom, weariness washed through me. I rocked from foot to foot to avoid passing out.

Hedrek brushed his beak against my thigh. "Take her home," he told Blake. "I'll collect Roya and the cats."

"But don't we want to leave Abel and Marika where they are?" I slurred my words and tried again. My second attempt was worse still, but everyone understood me.

"I will consider what they wish to do and make my own determination," Hedrek replied. "See you in Underhill."

One moment he was with us; the next he was gone.

Blake wrapped both arms around me. An infusion of power oozed down my spine. Not a lot, but enough to keep me sentient for the duration of our journey. "Help me understand," I murmured.

"Understand what, darling?"

"The Celts picked some no-name deity and stuck them with guarding the ley lines?"

He nodded. I felt the motion where I sagged against him. "Certainly seems so. Perhaps they promised her a short tenure to secure her cooperation. After all, Bodhmall had nothing else critical to do. Mostly, she tended a lavish flower garden and lush fields."

"When the agreed-upon brief stay turned to eternity, she complained," I hypothesized.

"Aye, and it was like as not when the hunt for you intensified," Blake concurred. He smoothed hair back from my face. "Rest, darling. We'll have time for whatever comes next."

"How? The Cait are still on the warpath."

He tilted my chin so my gaze met his. "Are they?"

I furrowed my forehead trying to think, but my brain

was mush. Too much had happened with too little sleep and food.

Blake's arms tightened around me. "You're daughter to the lines. The Celts may have created them, but they created you."

"Not following." My mind felt muzzy. It was tough to keep up with any train of thought for very long.

"The mage community was duped into believing you were the cause of malfunctions in the source of their power. We shall correct that misperception. Once you're ensconced in your rightful place as—"

"Hold up there." Suddenly, I was way more awake. "I'm an animal mage. It's all I ever wanted."

"You can be that too. And my mate, if you're still interested now that you've come into the full spectrum of your magic."

"What do you mean if? The person you fell in love with didn't go anywhere. I'm still right here." Aw crap. Did he not want me any longer? Had my primary allure been I was weaker than him magically? I took a ragged breath and asked, "Are you trying to wriggle out of your promises to me?"

"Oh hell, no. I'm not that easy to get rid of. I've fought for you Abria MacLeone. And I will continue to fight for you as long as I'm able."

Relief surged. I closed my arms around his body, holding on tight.

He laughed, the notes low, musical, soothing. Underhill formed around us, shading from passageways to Blake's rooms. Their familiar sense of peace surrounded me.

"We can sort all this out later." He chuckled. "For now, I'm going to lie down with you. We'll sleep until we're no longer tired, and then we'll eat. At some point, we'll clean up. We still reek of Hell's passageways."

If we did, I couldn't smell them anymore. Or maybe I could, but I'd adapted to the stench. "I want food first."

He smiled. "That could be arranged."

I reeled my confusion and far-ranging thoughts close to home. I'd sort out who I was later. For now, the simpler pursuits suited me fine.

I sat at a tiny table in Blake's kitchen, eating as if I'd never seen food before. I remember folding my arms on the table and resting my head on them, but I must have dozed because my next memory was lying next to Blake on soft sheepskins in front of one of the faux fires so popular in Underhill. He'd removed my filthy, stinking clothes, and the lush nap of the skins cradled me.

"Sleep, love. All is well."

Blake's words must have been spelled because the drop back into blackness was close to instantaneous.

CHAPTER 22
BLAKE

I kept watch over Abria, determined nothing would interrupt either her meal or her rest. A testament to her exhaustion was the way she'd fallen asleep at the table once her belly was full. Scooping her into my arms, I moved her to soft bedding in front of a fire and undressed her. The garments weren't worth salvaging.

Neither were mine. I considered a quick shower, but she and I would clean up together after she woke. I could have set warding around her, but it wasn't the same as me being here, front and center, to ensure her safety.

Savage protectiveness surged. Leaving her was out of the question.

Thank all the gods she hadn't broached the topic of her extended power. I wasn't certain what it meant, mostly because there's never been another like her. Surely, the lore books would yield information.

I couldn't cull through the library and remain by her

side. Kirwan or Breanne or any of my council would have gladly researched the topic, but until I knew more, I wasn't about to include anyone else in our recent discovery. I hadn't told Hedrek to keep his beak shut but trusted the owl to be circumspect. Working for Arianrhod—the virgin huntress who wasn't—he'd no doubt learned to hang onto secrets.

Besides, who would he tell? I had a feeling Arianrhod already possessed the full story about Abria's power. The other Celts must know as well. Anger rolled through me. Abria stirred in her sleep, moaning softly. I modulated my temper fast, lest my unrest translate somehow and break into her slumber.

Damn the Celts to Hell and back. How could they have been so remiss as to create Abria and leave her in the dark about the source of her power? And its magnitude. Their negligence was akin to sitting a curious child next to a bomb and hoping he didn't figure out how to detonate it.

Now that I knew where to look, the scope of Abria's ability humbled me. Someone had bound her talent with skill and stealth to hide it from her. Still, a mere thought could open the floodgates. Cailleach had pried them partway open. Arianrhod hadn't done much more. She hadn't had time, but I suspected she was ambivalent about the fallout if Abria were apprised of everything.

Once she knew how powerful she was, she could tell the whole world to bugger off—including them. And she could make the Cait's life into a swamp of misery. It was what I'd alluded to after her comment about them still being out for blood.

I'd have a heart-to-heart with the Celts. If I could locate them. But first, I needed to cool off. Abria's making could be as simple as them requiring a guardian for the ley lines. Or it might have been far more complex.

I've never trusted the Celts. They were rarely forthright with mages outside their ranks...

"You're back." Breanne's voice brushed my mind.

"Aye. Abria and me. Hedrek should show up any time with Roya and maybe a couple of cats."

"The Cait?" her mind voice shrilled.

"Nay. Garden-variety housecats. You recall our plan to infiltrate the Cait ranks."

After a long pause, she said, *"Council would like to know the outcome of your journey."*

I'm sure they would, an inner voice muttered dryly.

"I will call everyone together once I've fully rested."

"When will that be?"

I stifled a sigh. Now was a time to pull rank if ever there was one. *"I will let you know."* With that, I built wards around Abria and me. Under normal circumstances, I'm far more egalitarian, but until I chose a path regarding Abria and her magic, I needed time to sort the pros and cons.

Not that my people wouldn't sense her enhanced talents, but they'd assume she'd come by greater power courtesy of her years with Cailleach and her short stint with Arianrhod. In a backhanded way, she had.

I shut my eyes to rest them and pulled Abria closer. She nestled into my embrace making little cooing sounds that reminded me of a dove.

"HEY THERE, SLEEPYHEAD."

Her voice startled me. I rubbed my eyes. "Damn it. Hadn't planned to fall asleep."

She threaded fingers into my dirty, tangled hair. "You earned it. Don't know about you, but I feel ever so much better."

I smiled. Mission accomplished. "How about a bath? It's the one thing that didn't happen."

"I'll get it ready for us."

She covered my mouth with hers and kissed me. What began as something soft and tender turned passionate with the speed of light. She slid her tongue into my mouth, and I teased it with my own. We bit and sucked and licked until my cock thickened against her belly. Her nipples formed peaks pressing into my chest, and our breath came quickly.

With a single, fluid motion, she twisted away from me, landing on her feet. "You're enticing as they come, but we need that bath. I might not have smelled demons before, but I sure do now. Ewww." She crinkled her nose and sprinted for the door leading to the bathroom.

The place she'd lain against me felt cold, empty. I rolled to a sit and watched her hurry across the room. Her long legs and high ass were beautiful, her curved spine a work of art. The sound of water splashing into my oversized marble tub drove me to my feet. I was still tired, but I'd live.

The scents of rose and jasmine drifted through the open bathroom door. I padded that way, catching wafts of sulfur and ozone with every step. Turning, I sent a bit of power to clear any residual odor from the sheepskins. When I ducked into the steamy bathroom, Abria was stretched full length in the tub, hair floating around her like liquid fire.

I sat on the edge, dangling my feet in the water. "Room for me?"

"Always." She sat, and I slid in behind her. "I've been thinking," she murmured and settled against me.

"A dangerous enterprise," I teased. Grabbing one of many spray nozzles, I wetted my hair.

"Be serious." She repositioned herself so she faced me and grabbed a nozzle, aiming it at my chest.

I laughed. Two could play that game, and it might divert her from whatever she'd cooked up in that rapier-sharp mind of hers. I squirted water at her luscious breasts. She sprayed me back.

It wasn't the most efficient bath, but we laughed and squealed like a couple of schoolkids. As a corollary, we got clean and the irresistible urge to sink my unruly member inside her retreated—a little.

Council deserved an explanation.

Abria deserved something better than me sidestepping her earlier, "I've been thinking," comment.

And I deserved unbroken time in the Sidhe library. Of the three, it held the lowest priority.

The water's pretty murky." Abria slapped it with her hand.

I snorted. "Murky is kind. It's downright dingy. Come on." I hauled myself over the rim of the tub and offered her a hand. With the other I opened the drain.

"We can start with fresh once it's empty, right?" She

angled a russet brow before joining me on the gold-veined marble floor.

"Shower's quicker. We'll rinse off." I opened taps set into the wall, and we took turns standing under a sunflower shower head. Water sprayed all over the bathroom, but indwelling spells redirected and corralled it.

"Why are we in a rush?" She twisted the faucets to off, grabbed a towel, and tossed me one.

"The council needs me, but before I do that, what have you been thinking about?" I asked.

She frowned. "I had the strangest dreams. They got me to thinking."

"What kind of dreams?" We were dry, so I draped an arm around her and led us back into my bedchamber where several armoires held an assortment of clothes.

I handed her a pair of soft beige chamois trousers and an Irish-knit deep-blue sweater. "What happened to my things?" she asked.

"You're joking, right?" Ferreting about, I found black linen pants, a stretchy pale-green top, and a leather vest for myself.

She offered a sheepish grin and donned the garments. "Guess the old ones were about ready for the rubbish heap."

"If it makes you feel any better, mine got tossed too."

She was dressed. I wasn't. She circled behind me and wove her arms around my shoulders. Breasts pressed into my back. Her unique scent tantalized me. Vanilla, cinnamon, and wildflowers. My cock, which hadn't totally retreated, sprang to full attention in seconds.

A groan started in my belly and moved upward. I untangled her arms and turned to face her. "I'd like nothing better than to take our clean bodies back to bed and stay for a week."

She cocked her head to one side. "I'm up for two weeks even, but I hear a but."

"Aye, there is a big but. Council is awaiting me—and I want to hear about your dream. It might shed light on..." Uncertain what to say before I said too much, I stopped.

"On what?" She trained earnest liquid eyes on my face.

I couldn't hedge. This was the woman I loved, who I planned to spend forever with. We owed one another basic honesty. "On how your new role as daughter to the ley lines will play out."

Abria closed her teeth over her lower lip. "I've been wondering the same. I guess the fancy ability has always been there. The only difference is we know about it."

I shook my head.

"What?"

"Your enhanced power has been there all along. That part is correct, but you'd never have stumbled across it by accident. Someone went to a great deal of trouble to conceal it from everyone who didn't know precisely where to look."

"Didn't we already sort of know that?"

"Aye, but not the extent of what they hid from plain sight. Tell me about your dreams."

She squinched her eyes in thought. "There was only one, but it went on so long it felt like a movie. I was embroiled in the midst of an enormous battle. Warriors spread as far as I could see on all sides. I was at the head of a major army. I felt them arrayed behind me, sensed personal links to each of their power."

"Who was on the other side?" I cut in.

She made a chopping motion with one hand. "Let me get through this so I don't forget anything."

I nodded agreement and hurried into the clothes I'd laid out.

"I couldn't tell who we fought," she went on. "The enemy was shrouded in veils. Not individually, but they blocked a clear view of who they were." She shoved wet hair over her shoulders.

"The worst part was everyone looked to me, assumed I was some kind of whiz at commanding troops. I've never done anything like it before. Why would I know how? Anyway, Becca showed up, and—"

"The unicorn?" So much for my promise to remain silent.

"Yeah. She swept me onto her back, and we took off across a mud-choked field like a latter day Joan of Arc. An enormous stag with golden horns ran next to us. One by one, we vanished into the veils—or the mist. Since I was at the front of the line, I got sucked in first. It was unbelievably cold and pitch black. Evil pressed down on us from all sides. It almost sapped all hope from me, but Becca kept going. So did the stag."

Abria dropped her head into her hands. I wrapped my arms around her, murmuring, "Only a dream, darling."

She shook her head. "It was far more than that. It was a true sending of the future. Must be the future because I've never done anything like that in the past."

"Is there more?"

"Not really. It disturbed me so much, I clawed my way back here. Pretty sure I slept some more after that."

"What do you want to do right now?"

"You already nixed my top choice."

"Which was?"

"Fucking each other's brains out." She winked broadly.

I laughed. "It's only on hold for the moment. Hang on to that thought, wench. I won't be gone too long at council. We put off the mating ceremony. I'd like to plan for it in the next couple of days."

"Are you sure? Looks like trouble will follow me wherever I go. You have a realm to manage."

"Very sure." I kissed her forehead then both cheeks and her mouth. "I love you, darling."

"I love you too, but you could take your pick of the Sidhe. Find someone with far less baggage."

I placed a finger over her lips. "You're who I want. Maybe you could figure out who's coming to our wedding. We have a wardrobe room on one of the lower levels. Feel free to cull through it. I'm sure you'll find clothing that fits to replace what I threw away."

"I already came up with a guest list. Remember? Last chance to back out."

"After all the trouble it was get you to say yes, there aren't words in the universe that would talk me out of it."

"This might come back to haunt you." A corner of her mouth twitched with amusement.

"I'll take my chances."

She walked into my arms. I held her, breathing her in.

When she stretched on tiptoe and kissed me, I kissed her back. Caught between duty to the Sidhe and the magic of the woman pressed against me, I chose Abria.

Her fingers kneaded my back, leaving trails of heat and need before dropping lower to grasp my hips. "What about the council?" she murmured between kisses.

"They've waited this long."

"We'll be quick." She hip butted me.

"One day, wench, we'll have all the time in the world." I backed us toward the bed.

"One day," she agreed. "Until then, I'll take what I can get."

She made me laugh. "I like my women pragmatic."

"Oh, I'm as pragmatic as they come." Her pants pooled around her ankles, and she stepped out of them.

We'd reached the bed. I slid my trousers out of the way, sat on its edge, and drew her onto my lap.

You've reached the end of *Hunted*, third of the Wayward Mage books if you count the prequel, *Hands of Fate*. Abria and Blake's story continues in *Salvaged*. While you're thinking about it, please leave a review for *Hunted*. Doesn't have to be fancy. A line or two will do it to let others know how much you're enjoying this series.

See you soon with *Salvaged* to close out this series.

BOOK DESCRIPTION: SALVAGED

Life used to be so simple. I solved cases for mortals, earning myself a solid reputation as a crack detective. And I basked in the adoration of every animal, bird, and sea creature known to Western man. The animal mage part is the same, but everything else has changed.

The last time I remember being happy was the day I married Blake. Since then, nothing has gone right. When he met me, I traveled beneath crossed stars. Jinxed is a kind term for the trouble that followed me.

He says we're stronger together, but I'm starting to doubt that. Some challenges are meant to be faced alone. Maybe I can fix the problems plaguing us. Maybe I can't, but I have to try.

And I must do it with my animal allies. Blake won't like any of it, which means I'll have to slip away when he's not paying attention. And I'll have to cover my tracks well to make sure he doesn't follow me.

He's my heart, my life, but if I don't leave him, he'll be doomed right along with me, and I refuse to let that happen.

SALVAGED, CHAPTER ONE, ABRIA

"You're out of nuts," Hedrek hooted from the vicinity of my tiny kitchen.

I looked up from my computer screen. "So? Go hunting."

He's a magical owl, many times bigger than your average barn owl. And one of my self-appointed protectors. Maybe not exactly self-appointed. Arianrhod, Celtic goddess and virgin huntress, had tasked him with my safety. But that had been a while ago. Neither of us had seen her since before I tackled the ley lines—and fixed them.

He flew into my study and perched on the edge of my desk. "It's not exactly safe for you to be here. I am not leaving."

I gave up on any catchup for my private detective business. I hadn't taken a client for months, but people were still emailing. Gave me hope of resurrecting something viable. But I couldn't concentrate with Hedrek nattering in one ear.

"What do you want to do?" I asked him.

"Return to Underhill. We're already much later than I promised Blake."

A sigh rattled from me. Once I'd been a free agent, totally on my own. Now I had a phalanx of babysitters. "Can you give me another half hour? Please." I moved from behind the monitor, smiled at the tawny owl with golden eyes, and added, "How about a few crackers? They're probably stale, but food is food."

"Meat?" A hopeful note feathered under the one word.

"Look in the freezer."

He turned and flew back the way he'd come. I returned to my texts and emails. Electronics don't work in Underhill. Something about the energy of the Faery realm defeats the electromagnetic waves that power phones and tablets.

Blake hadn't been pleased about me returning to my home in Nairn. He'd insisted on sweeping the place to make certain it wasn't magically booby-trapped. It must have passed because he'd grudgingly allowed as to how I could access my home again.

A series of thumps from the kitchen suggested Hedrek had found what he sought. I hoped he didn't make too big a mess on my scarred wooden floor, but at least he'd be occupied for a while.

I hadn't spent five minutes with my correspondence before magical currents announced someone's imminent arrival. I shot to my feet, hands extended, defensive power balanced between them. If something bad happened here, Blake would probably torch the place. At least then I could collect on the insurance.

I don't exactly need money anymore, not with all the wealth of Faery standing behind me as Blake's intended. But old habits die hard.

Hedrek blasted into the room in a whirlwind of feathers with something bloody hanging out of his curved beak. Dropping his prize on my rug, where it was sure to leave a nasty stain, he said, "Someone is near. We're leaving."

"Shall we see who it is first?" I kept my voice even. Just because everyone else in my current universe was fussed up about my safety, I refused to live like that.

Hedrek landed in front of me, wings spread. "But I have to answer to Arianrhod," he protested.

A gateway formed near my front door, glowing blue-white. I'd know that magical signature anywhere. Leaping to my feet, I skirted the owl and hurried forward. "It's okay," I told Hedrek. "It's just Birgit."

With a flurry of huffing noises that weren't especially owl-like at all, he retreated to the glob he'd dropped. Too bad he didn't have the kind of tongue that would lick up the blood.

The gateway glowed brighter. I opened my arms as Birgit stepped through. About my height and wraith thin, she'd always reminded me of a raptor wearing human skin. Her hair was white and plaited into two thick braids that hung down her back. Ice-blue eyes regarded me from beneath white brows. Her face was all planes and angles with a sharp beak of a nose and a thin-lipped mouth.

Today, she was smiling as she walked into my embrace. "So good to see you," she announced before stepping back.

"You as well. How about a cup of tea?"

"I'd love one, but don't you have things to do? It's your wedding day, child."

I made a face. "Gah. Don't remind me. It's why I'm here. I had to get out of Underhill. Everyone was driving me nuts with all the preparations. And Blake is so nervous, I wonder if he won't back out at the last minute."

We walked into the kitchen with Hedrek trailing behind us. Good thing since he'd left the freezer door wide open and an assortment of packages of frozen meat strewn across the floor. I bent to pick them up.

"Not done yet," he croaked.

A staunch meow preceded a hefty black tomcat jumping out of somewhere in Birgit's deep green robe. He landed on the floor and rolled one of the packages over with a paw before turning to the owl. "Mind if we share?" Jethro purred fetchingly.

Tough to refuse him anything when he purred like that. He's a Sidhe seer who spends most of him time in cat form. He and Birgit go back a long way.

I put the kettle on. Hedrek picked up one of the frozen packets and pushed it Jethro's way. Rearing back on his haunches, the cat mimed a bow before ripping paper off the frozen whatever it was.

"So how are you feeling?" Birgit inquired once I'd poured boiling water over a combination of mint, anise, and rosemary.

"About?"

She pursed her lips into a thin line. "Don't be disingenuous with me, dearie."

Busted.

"Wasn't trying to be. Not on purpose, anyway," I replied. "I love Blake, but he comes with so much baggage."

She cackled. "Oh. You mean the rest of the Sidhe?"

I nodded. "And his responsibility to them."

"Is it you who's thinking about backing out?"

Her question caught me where I live. I considered my answer carefully. "No. Not exactly. He and I are meant to be together, but trouble lies ahead. A lot of it. I'd prefer if he were safe, and I'll be damned if I implicate the Sidhe in my problems."

Birgit drew her white brows together. "But you fixed the ley lines. Are other mages still after you?"

I set my cup down and pinched the bridge of my nose between a thumb and forefinger. "Not sure who's after me, but someone is."

She spun a hand. "Tell me."

"Nothing specific. Not really, but I keep having these fucking dreams where I'm riding at the head of an army. It's me and Becca and this golden stag, and—"

"Whoa. A golden stag, you say?" At my nod, she went on. "You're dreaming of the Hunt, child."

My eyes widened. "The Wild Hunt? But that's straight out of Norse mythology."

"Your point?" Birgit's blue gaze drilled into me.

I shrugged. "Not my pantheon."

"If you're dreaming about the stag, it certainly is." She leaned against the back of her chair. "Once the wedding is past, we need to investigate. I know Odin, and—"

"Blake isn't going to like this," I muttered.

"'Tisn't for him to judge," she said tartly. "But you might hold off on telling him until after the ceremony."

"He already knows," I said dully. "And he didn't breathe a word about the Norse gods."

Her rugged features mirrored confusion. "But surely he must know the significance of the stag."

I got to my feet and ferried our mugs to the sink. Since I was close to the cold box, I closed the freezer door. It appeared all the frozen meat was well on its way down furred and feathered gullets. I'd clear away the wrappings later.

"We should go back," I muttered.

"About time." Hedrek looked up from his meal.

"Where's your dress?" Birgit asked.

"It's a tunic and pants. Everything is in Underhill."

She was on her feet. Coming close, she wrapped her arms around me. "It will be better than you believe."

"What will be?" My voice was muffled against her shoulder.

"Why your future. Yours and Blake's. Jethro's seen snatches of it."

A deep purr corroborated her statement.

Part of me was still considering simply vanishing, but it would break Blake's heart. Unfortunately, it would shatter mine as well. No way out but through, which isn't how most gals approach their wedding day.

I left the cups in the sink and turned off my computer. By the time I was done, Birgit was standing by the remnants of her portal with Jethro in her arms and Hedrek next to her. I joined them and we walked through the witch's gateway into Underhill near the council chamber.

"Neat trick," I told her.

"Bests teleporting for short trips," she agreed.

Short trips, eh? "I had no idea my place in Nairn was anywhere near Underhill," I mumbled.

"It wasn't, but Blake fixed that."

I resisted rolling my eyes. Of course, he would have.

"I'll see you later today," Hedrek informed me and squeezed through Birgit's portal just as it was closing. He had magic aplenty to bend it to his will.

"You're not ready yet." Breanne's tone held censure as she hustled toward us. Tall and broad, were it not for breasts, she'd have been built like a linebacker.

"I have time," I protested.

"Precious little," she retorted and made shooing motions as if I were a chicken or something.

I took a good look at her. Her usual battle axe was absent, and she was wearing something decidedly feminine for her: a cream-colored robe trimmed in lace and sashed in deep blue. White hair curled around her face, and her grey eyes sparked with unusual excitement.

"Hurry." She gave me a little shove.

"Get dressed," Birgit suggested. "Breanne and I can catch up."

A reprieve! I didn't wait around but hustled to the rooms I share with Blake. I hadn't expected him to be there, and he wasn't. The door opened obligingly as soon as I got close to it. That was something new.

Someone had laid my finery out on a low table near the

bed. I shucked my pants and sweatshirt, stood under the shower for a few moments, and was drying off when I heard Blake's footsteps.

He poked his head into the steamy bathroom. Every time I look at him, my heart stutters and breath catches in my throat. I may fuss and fume about how he hovers over me, but he is the most breathtaking man I've ever laid eyes on. Today, in his wedding garments, he was even more stunning. Dark hair brushed his shoulders. His eyes were dark liquid pools, and black wings set with jewels folded across his back. He's a wee bit taller than me, with the body of a Greek god.

The warmth from his smile sank into my soul. "There you are." His voice was deep, rich, melodic. "I'd been wondering if you changed your mind."

I hung the towel over a hook and walked into his open arms. The silk of his moss green robe tantalized my naked flesh. He hugged me and nuzzled my neck. I wrapped my arms around him, luxuriating in the play of bone and muscle beneath my fingertips.

The swell of his erection butted into my belly. I reached between us to cup him in a hand. "Do we have time?"

He disentangled us, one from the other. "Unfortunately, no, my love."

I gave his cock one more squeeze before letting go. "Too bad."

"Hang onto that thought. There's always after the ceremony. When everyone expects us to disappear."

I felt his gaze on me as I pulled a pair of soft brown linen trousers over my legs. A white long-sleeved tunic hand embroidered with runes followed. I rustled through my jewelry box and withdrew a five-carat square-cut emerald suspended from a golden chain. Blake fastened it around my neck.

My usual boots or running shoes wouldn't do at all. Someone had placed a pair of strappy sandals next to the bed. I slid them on and buckled them.

"You never answered me," Blake said.

I'd moved on to brushing out my long hair. "About what?"

"Second thoughts?"

My cheeks warmed, a dead giveaway that meant I couldn't twist the truth. I looked up from where I perched on the edge of the bed. "Of course, I thought about dropping out of sight. Trouble follows me wherever I go. I'm not happy about involving you or your people."

"You can't know the future. Besides, if the Sidhe were at war—and technically, we still are with our Cait cousins— you wouldn't have abandoned me."

Ouch. Point taken.

I got to my feet and walked to where he waited for me near the door. "I do love you, Blake. Never doubt it."

He tucked my hand between both of his. "I don't. We're stronger together, Abria. I waited a long time for you." His smile drilled through all my reservations. "You are the most beautiful, most fetching, unbelievably gorgeous woman I've ever known."

I grinned. "Admit it. You love me for my rapier-sharp wit and inquiring mind."

"That too." He let go and offered his arm. "Shall we?"

I nodded and the heady scents of the natural world bombarded me as he transported us to a deserted stretch of beach off the highway north of Nairn. I'd first met Cailleach there, and we'd selected it as a perfect spot for our nuptials since it meant the mer-people, seals, walruses, and fish could join all the other animals and share our joy.

We emerged in a shower of white sparks. Everyone was already here; cheers rose from Sidhe throats. Hundreds of animals, birds, and sea creatures surged forward, surrounding me with hoots, caws, honks, purrs, squeals, and yips.

Arianrhod, Ceridwen, and Cailleach waited on the beach with a fire burning between them. A triumvirate of crones and their holy flames.

We walked forward until we stood a meter away facing them with the fire between us.

Birgit flanked me on my right side with Jethro strutting next to her.

Kirwan flanked Blake.

I've never attended a Sidhe wedding. Why would I have? In truth, I can count the weddings I've been part of through my 700 plus years on the fingers of one hand.

Chanting rose from the goddesses creating runes in the gusty marine air. For once, the sun was out, but it didn't surprise me. Power untold was arrayed in front of us. Surely, they could hold back Scotland's continual bleak weather for a short while.

Blake vowed everything a groom usually does, but his words bound him with blood and magic. I promised him everything in return, mirroring his words. Cailleach made long cuts in our forearms. Where our blood joined, it created multihued streamers that floated around us before being absorbed in the fire.

So that was why it was there.

Blood gives our enemies power over us. The goddesses weren't taking any chances. If darkness stalked this beach once we were gone, there'd be aught to harvest.

It might have been the chanting or the singing or the runes or the blood, but the last of my reservations fell away. I couldn't imagine my life without Blake. And then he was kissing me, and people were yelling bawdy suggestions and mobbing us. Everyone wanted a kiss or a hug or a word.

The wound on my arm closed as if it had never been there. Likewise, the rent in my tunic vanished.

Animals wormed their way through the Sidhe, determined to wish me, their queen, well. Equally determined to thank each and every one of them, I pushed through the crowed and took up a spot on a large flat rock. At some point, Blake joined me.

The sun was edging toward the western horizon when the last of my retinue faded away. Someone placed goblets of mead into our hands and toasted our marriage. We repaired to caves set into the cliffs where tables teemed with delicacies.

Blake tapped my shoulder. "It's been five minutes," he said around a mouthful of something-or-other.

"Since?" I chewed and swallowed the last of a piece of a quiche-like delicacy.

"Anyone's come over," he clarified. "I don't want to tear you away from your wedding, but we could leave anytime."

"You're about as subtle as a steam engine, bud." I arched both brows. "Where are we going?"

"It's a surprise."

I clapped my hands together, feeling young and carefree. It wouldn't last, so I was determined to enjoy it while I could. "A honeymoon?"

"Nothing that elaborate, but I did carve out a private spot for us outside of Underhill."

"Oooh. Where?"

In answer, he scooped me into his arms and ignited a travel spell he must have had at the ready. When it cleared, we were in an elaborate, old-fashioned bedchamber in what appeared to be a castle.

He put me down, and I strode to expansive windows overlooking lush grounds. A lake below had several pairs of swans swimming this way and that.

Blake wrapped his arms around me from behind. "Do you like it?"

I turned and hugged him. "I love it."

"Good." He beamed at me. "Sometimes my other life as Earl of Galloway comes in handy. This is Castle Douglas. I rented the whole thing for a few days. Just for us."

I nestled against him. "We could have gone back to Underhill."

He stroked my hair. "We could have, but I wanted something special. And somewhere we'd be left alone."

Love for the man in my arms surged, filling me with such strong emotions I could scarcely contain them. I'm sure they spilled out this way and that as Blake settled his mouth over mine.

Lost in the power whirling around us, I opened my mouth to his questing tongue.

Sex is the easy part, an inner voice warned. I shushed it and went to work divesting my brand new husband of his clothing.

ABOUT THE AUTHOR

Ann Gimpel is a USA Today bestselling author. A lifelong aficionado of the unusual, she began writing speculative fiction a few years ago. Since then her short fiction has appeared in many webzines and anthologies. Her longer books run the gamut from urban fantasy to paranormal romance. Once upon a time, she nurtured clients. Now she nurtures dark, gritty fantasy stories that push hard against reality. When she's not writing, she's in the backcountry getting down and dirty with her camera. She's published over 100 books to date, with several more planned for 2022 and beyond. A husband, grown children, grandchildren, and wolf hybrids round out her family.

Keep up with her at www.anngimpel.com or http://anngimpel.blogspot.com

If you enjoyed what you read, get in line for special offers and pre-release special reads. Newsletter Signup!

ALSO BY ANN GIMPEL

SERIES

Alphas in the Wild

Hello Darkness

Alpine Attraction

A Run for Her Money

Fire Moon

Bitter Harvest

Deceived

Twisted

Abandoned

Betrayed

Redeemed

Cataclysm

Harsh Line

Warped Line

Cracked Line

Broken Line

Circle of Assassins

Shira

Quinn

Rhiana

Kylian

Grigori

Magick and Misfits

Court of Rogues

Midnight Court

Court of the Fallen

Court of Destiny

Coven Enforcers

Blood and Magic

Blood and Sorcery

Blood and Illusion

Demon Assassins

Witch's Bounty

Witch's Bane

Witches Rule

Dragon Heir

Dragon's Call

Dragon's Blood

Dragon's Heir

Dragon Lore

Highland Secrets

To Love a Highland Dragon

Dragon Maid

Dragon's Dare

Dragon Fury

Earth Reclaimed

Earth's Requiem

Earth's Blood

Earth's Hope

Elemental Witch

Timespell

Time's Curse

Time's Hostage

Gatekeeper

Shadow Reaper

Rebel Reaper

Untamed Reaper

GenTech Rebellion

Winning Glory

Honor Bound

Claiming Charity

Loving Hope

Keeping Faith

Ice Dragon

Feral Ice

Cursed Ice

Primal Ice

Magick and Misfits (Fall and Winter 2020)

Court of Rogues

Midnight Court

Court of the Fallen

Court of Destiny

Rubicon International

Garen

Lars

Soul Dance

Tarnished Beginnings

Tarnished Legacy

Tarnished Prophecy

Tarnished Journey

Soul Storm

Dark Prophecy

Dark Pursuit

Dark Promise

Underground Heat

Roman's Gold

Wolf Born

Blood Bond

Wayward Mage

Hands of Fate

Jinxed

Hunted'

Salvaged

Wolf Clan Shifters

Alice's Alphas

Megan's Mates

Sophie's Shifters

Wylde Magick

Gemstone

Lion's Lair

Unbalanced

STANDALONE BOOKS

Branded, That Old Black Magic Romance (paranormal romance)

Edge of Night (short story collection, paranormal and horror)

Grit is a 4-Letter Word (nonfiction)

Heart's Flame (post-apocalyptic romance)

Icy Passage (science fiction romance)

Marked by Fortune (post-apocalyptic coming of age story)

Melis's Gambit (historical paranormal romance)

Midnight Magic (paranormal romance)

Red Dawn (post-apocalyptic paranormal romance)

Shadow Play (historical paranormal romance)

Shadows in Time (Highland time travel romance)

Since We Fell (contemporary romance)

Warin's War (paranormal romance)